GEARS

A COLLECTION

ALEX M. PRUTEANU

Published by Independent Talent Group, Inc.
Fairlawn, Ohio 44333
gearscollection@gmail.com

Designed by Teresa Chapman

Illustrations by Teresa Chapman, Gillian Pruteanu, Alex M. Pruteanu

Cover Image Title: *Reproduction of page from notebook of Leonardo da Vinci showing
a geared device assembled and disassembled*
Reproduction Number: LC-USZ62-110332
Repository: Library of Congress Washington, D.C. 20540 USA

ISBN-13: 978-0-9840093-2-9

Printed in the United States of America

PRAISE FOR GEARS

"*Gears* is an unforgettable collection that strikes a match, lighting up the shadows of Gogol and Vonnegut in more than a few raucous smokes together. Pruteanu is a master of language, character and submersion. *Gears* is deep waters.
Get ready to go under."

–Meg Tuite, author of *Domestic Apparition and Implosion*

"In his first collection, Pruteanu delivers a series of fictitious 'cogs' which grind together and move forward with the momentum and impact of a speeding freight train. Reminiscent of Kafka and Camus and even the great Russian novelists, Pruteanu displays that rarest ability to create believable and entertaining allegory, while at the same time deftly omitting crucial elements, allowing the reader to interpret his or her own meaning. The result is a series of machinations on love and death, oppression and adversity, identity and purpose; in effect, the machine strips away our options—and the world opens up."

–Pat Pujolas, author of *Jimmy Lagowski Saves The World*

"Reading Pruteanu, you can't help but imagine a big-hearted and wild-eyed writer on the end of the line, one of the rare few who gives a damn. His writing makes you feel less strange and less alone, not an easy trick to pull off."

–James A. Reeves, author of *The Road to Somewhere:*
An American Memoir

"Reading Alex Pruteanu's *Gears* is like taking refuge in a restroom in the Denver airport during a tornado warning, and meeting a weirdly enchanting exile who tells stories and word puzzles that remind you that the spinning vortices of life are inside as well as outside: sometimes they are on the scale of clouds and states, and other times they are the size and shape of the subtlest contradictions."

–Christopher Schaberg, author of *The Textual Life of Airports:*
Reading the Culture of Flight

for Teresa

ACKNOWLEDGMENTS

Thank you to the dozens of editors of the literary journals in which most of these 'gears' originally appeared. I am grateful that you took a chance publishing sometimes controversial, sometimes foreign, but always (I think) dynamic subjects that I explore and present in my writing.

CONTENTS

GEARS

GEARS

FOREWORD

I have always been fascinated by components working together to form a whole. Whether or not that whole is efficient does not matter to me; in fact, the more inefficient the more interesting, because that means its parts may be flawed. Nor is this fascination with parts necessarily mechanical.

I am intrigued by how political and social systems are subdivided, how labor is delegated to different sections within a corporation, how society itself arranges its many parts in its many boxes (caste systems, social strata, etc.).

The stories in this collection, I feel, act very much like cogs in the Machine that is the book itself. In every short story that you will read here, there is a type of movement, whether physical or ethereal, implied or described.

As with any complex system, I feel there are the myriad details, the gears that move within the guts of the process itself. It's often times that those gears are doing much more interesting work than the Machine; think about: what frantic activity goes on inside our bodies while we indolently sit on our couch and veg out in front of the flat screen.

But in this case, I hope you do find the work and purpose of the Machine as interesting as the activity of its gears.

A Sort of Love Letter to ~~Elise Mother~~ The State
(Jumping Blue Gods, May 2012)

March XX, XXXX

My Dearest,

I have not missed you. I realize how ghastly that may sound after thirty-two years of not seeing one another, but you insisted (with your instruments) in teaching me not to lie. And so. You were always such an exquisite contradiction; from the basements and secret chambers in which you did your work, later worshipping and lighting candles for the dignified calmness of the reposed lying at your calloused feet, to the folds of your silk, imported skirt hiding those horrible nocturnal surprises. Often I tried to look up your vestments, searching for a glimpse of thigh or even something else, a bit higher, a bit more forbidden, but there was never any getting past the sentinel or the hematic barbed wire.

I would wish to say that I am well and well adjusted in this new land; that I have started a family and have continued the path of the dream which has been laid out for me...ultimately by you. I would wish to say that. But every sweet William I see sounds like a sad and lucky song written for you and I; a map of both of us in bare feet, without a bra, standing on a frigid floor below ground level. Me before you.

I have you to thank under my fingertips; you: a girl wanting to jump, and me: a boy obsessed with cannibalism and singed flesh. You: the Miriam, daughter of Amram and Jochebed, wanting to keep and nurse me by the side of the river first, before letting me go. Me: a feeble Hebrew boy doomed by the orders of the Pharaoh.

I could count the days since last I saw you, since last I moved your clothes out of my closet...but in the three decades that have passed I have become busy creating lists of songs by dead singers who knew what I felt before I knew what I felt, and before we could tell one another what we felt.

At times, I think you wish for me to find you. I think you wish for me to seethe with jealousy at your perpetual engagement with men who live in salt mines; with men who cannot grow teeth any longer; with whispers. I feel your macabre pull oozing from the walls, like feedback from hidden microphones grinning at betrayal and the broken spirit of an ordinary man.

Oh, but you have always been such an exquisite contradiction.

Good morning to you, my sweet addiction.
Goodnightgoodmorning.

Resident Alien
(Used Furniture Review, July 2012)

I was born in the middle of the day, in the middle of the week, in the middle of the year, in the middle of the twentieth century. I checked in screaming and gurgling, bloody red and violet with revolt and anger. What I really wanted to do was to delay everything by nineteen years, so I could be held up to the window looking at the moon while Armstrong lowered his foot into the powdery surface and uttered those famous words about small steps and giant steps. But I didn't have the call on that. I came when I came.

The man who delivered me named me, in spite of my mother's wishes. I was meant to be christened after Saint Paul. Instead, the obstetrician, who had a limited knowledge of history but a passion for chess and Ottoman Empire coffee, declared me a world conqueror. But what he didn't realize in his atheist, intellectual pseudo-statement was that he named me for a saint after all. There are so many of them, you're bound to hit a target if you just merely chuck the rock.

My mother, after being handed the blue and bloody baby, immediately asked for a cigarette. And then she held me to her breast, as was customary and to save face, because I was ugly. I had a crooked nose. It was almost fused to the left side of my cheekbone from having passed through the birth canal obtusely, in a hard, twenty-six-hour labour. In the coming weeks my father would *exercise* my snout, bending it first toward the opposite side, then slowly back to the center. Eventually it would be straight. And big. I took my paternal grandfather's Greek proboscis. My father would claim victory over the defect. Victory through persistence and practice. My father would claim many things.

"Give me a cigarette, Yuri!"

Yuri, the obstetrician who delivered me was a substitute—on call that Wednesday afternoon. The man in whose prenatal care my mother had been entrusted by the government the last thirty-nine weeks was on holiday at the Black Sea. At the moment I presented myself smeared in fetoplacental circulatory blood and matter, he was rolling a double-six on the backgammon board at a café in the coastal town of Eforie. His opponent, a Turk from Izmir who sold fur pelts from a kiosk at night, and corn on the cob from a steaming bucket during the hot days on the beach, had just raised the odds to 32. The instant double-sixes had settled on the board, I wailed with my first breath in a sterile room, two hundred kilometers to the west.

And that's when my mother insisted on having a Kent.

—

I had fluid in my lungs. But there was nothing they could do about it save holding me upside down a few minutes every hour, letting the yellowish substance trickle down. Nowadays they call the condition Transient Tachypnea of the Newborn, and if you happen to check in with it, they stick all kinds of tubes down your throat and take blood samples every four hours, pricking your little, newborn heels and squeezing the drops into a vile.

After they wiped me down, they took me away, and my mother and father did not see me for three weeks. During her recovery, my mother ate fatty chicken soup with pieces of skin floating in the bowl.

My father was a good cook. He had learned basic peasant cooking techniques living eighteen years in his birth village in the northeast, just on the border with the U.S.S.R. He'd learned how to make polenta with chunks of head cheese, and stuff ground meat into pork casings as a boy, to help out his mother who would have to deal with her abusive, alcoholic husband most nights. Later my father would eat the same greasy broth, as he lay in a hospital bed with half his colon cut away by a negligent doctor.

In the weeks that the hospital cared for me, giving me oxygen and continuous positive airway pressure, my mother learned how to fold and wash diapers in icy cold water, tightly swaddle a baby despite excruciatingly hot July weather, and from the pediatrician assigned to her by the state, she dutifully noted that, in order to keep me on schedule and under control, she should insert suppositories into my rectum every four to six hours.

—

My Greek maternal grandfather was called Xenofon Panaides. He was a strange, tall, Renaissance man trapped in the wrong half of the century, in the wrong country. He worked for decades in quality control at a rivets factory in Ploesti before the Allies bombed the refineries of the city in 1942. He was a daydreamer before the world had heard of Walter Mitty. He played himself in chess during his lunch breaks on a small, foldable board he had manufactured out of old shoeboxes and fabric in his outdoor kitchen, with pieces he had carved out of wood every Sunday for sixteen months. He taught himself English from old Hornby books, and had begun the daunting task of translating every work by Shakespeare into Romanian—for his own pleasure. He wrote short plays and stories, the manuscripts of which he kept in a large box under his bed and which no one read while he was alive. (Hardly anyone read them after he died.) He studied the violin and could play Rimsky-Korsakov's "Flight of the Bumblebee" with amazing speed and accuracy. He adored Herbert von Karajan and often listened to his beloved phonograph record of the Vienna Philharmonic's version of "Faust." But what grandfather Panaides loved the most was photography. Later, as a retired man slowly worked down by lung cancer, he would wake up at four in the morning, get on his bicycle, and pedal furiously out of town to catch the sunrise over the still charred oil fields at Brazi. Once, he got as far as Targoviste for a shot which he later over developed in his improvised darkroom. He failed to mix a proper stop bath and when he poured the working solution into the developing tank, the solution failed to neutralize the developer and arrest the developing process.

—

When I was almost six, he taught me the Latvian Gambit:

1. e4 e5

2. Nf3 f5

At this point several possible moves by White have been studied, of which the most important are:

3. Nxe5 – the main line. Now after the usual 3...Qf6 (3...Nc6?!, the so-called "Corkscrew Counter Gambit," is also known, to which 4.d4! is a good response), White chooses between 4. d4 d6 5. Nc4 fxe4 and the immediate 4. Nc4, which has the advantage of allowing White to open the center with d3, for example 4...fxe4 5.Nc3 Qg6?! 6.d3 exd3? 7. Bxd3 Qxg2? and now White is winning after 8. Qh5 + Kd8 (or 8...g6 9. Qe5 + and 10. Be4) 9. Be4.

(Twenty-eight years later, American grandmaster Joel Benjamin will claim that this sensible developing move refutes the Latvian:

3. exf5

3. d4)

In his outdoor kitchen on a shelf high above the stove, grandfather Panaides had an impossibly thick book of problems, combinations, and games edited by Polgár. The few times he hauled it down and allowed me to thumb through it very carefully and methodically, I smelled mildew and bacon rising off the yellow, delicate pages. The acrid odor made me sneeze every time. In the unabridged chess bible, I came across the names of Mikhail Botvinnik, Samuel Reshevsky, Herman Steiner, Arthur Bisquier, and a strange American named Robert Fischer.

In May, 1949 the six-year-old Fischer learned how to play

chess from instructions found in a chess set that was bought at a candy store below his Brooklyn apartment. He saw his first chess book a month later. For over a year he played chess on his own. At age seven, he began to play chess seriously, joining the Brooklyn Chess Club and receiving instruction from its president, Carmine Nigro.

In June, 1955 Grandfather Panaides taught me the Latvian Gambit. And across the Atlantic Ocean, in a country, which Grandfather Panaides had loved ever since he was a boy, but which he would never see in his lifetime, Bobby Fischer joined the Manhattan Chess Club, one of the strongest in the world.

—

My other grandfather, dad's dad, couldn't grasp the reasonable and beautiful logic of chess. The head wounds he'd suffered in World War II as an infantryman left him with the inability to see or understand the diagonal, and so the Bishop, the Queen, and the King were rendered useless. As well, the *en passant*. Dad's dad was conscripted into the Romanian army on 29 November, 1940—just four days after the country joined the Axis by signing the Tripartite Pact. In July, 1941 during a break in action on the Eastern front, his helmet off, he straightened himself out of the trench to light a cigarette. The Russian sniper bullet came in from the forest line, a kilometer away, and had it been a few millimeters lower dad's dad would've taken his last breath on earth inhaling a shitty Marasesti cigarette. The second time he was clipped by a deadly piece of lead was in May, 1944 at the Battle of Targul Frumos when the Romanians were forced to switch sides and become allies of the Soviets. This time the bullet took out a piece of skull and left a trench running from the top of his forehead to the back of the head. Thus dad's dad had the only distinction of being shot twice in the head by either warring side, and having survived both times.

Though dad's dad couldn't grasp the rules of chess, he excelled at backgammon—a game I finally learned at the age of thirty-five, living in Damascus, Maryland with a woman who had been in such a horrific car accident that the imprint of the Pontiac's steering wheel insignia was visible on her sternum two years after the awful wreck. She and I played endless best-of-seven tournaments, while she was convalescing.

—

Grandfather Panaides loved dark chocolate. Every time he came to Bucharest to stay and visit with us in the small flat he brought a thick bar just for me. Chocolate, especially the dark kind, was extremely expensive and very hard to find in those times (any basic food was), and so he deduced that its rareness and exceptional quality would make the perfect (semi) sweet present for a child. I hated it. I barely tolerate it now. But I was told, via a leather belt to the thighs, to make concessions. We all lived within concessions then.

My country was a land of contradictions. We did not have water three days per week, yet we owned a West German Water-Pik. (In spite of that I had the most horrendous cavities as a child and later, in America, would need months of painful, follow-up work for crowns and bridges and root canals, coincidentally done by Dr. Janas, a Greek immigrant living comfortably in Elyria, Ohio and a friend of a friend of my pediatrician in Bucharest.)

We did not have religion (the State was officially atheist) but we went to church every Christmas and Easter eve and held lit candles in silent vigil alongside hundreds of faithful followers. Our priests were secret police informers, but were trusted with even the basic secrets like showing up for mass (men of cloth kept detailed notes on who was present at their sermons).

The government required every citizen to be a member of the Communist Party, yet both my parents didn't carry party cards. They had fallen through a loophole, which allowed all students from age six to be part of a socialist pioneer youth union—and when they finished their higher studies at university, they fell through the bureaucratic cracks of the Communist system via membership in a student socialist labour movement, and never officially graduated into the Party.

There were dozens and dozens more contradictions like that and we lived among all of them, traversing and hopping around and on them like frogs playing hopscotch on lily pads. The one that makes me laugh even now is our car. We owned a sparkling new Dacia 1300, a Renault knockoff, which basically stood parked on the street under a canvas cover, weathered with yellow and grey stains, for years. My father took out the battery the day the car was bought, and placed it under the sink in our kitchen where it lived until he and I emigrated. We had no food, but we had a brand new car, which we never used. Many things made no sense. But we accepted them. We lived in the absurd, which rendered us cynical but forgiving. It also instilled in us a fantastic sense of humour, although it seems something was lost in the transmission between generations and I ended up basically unable to deliver even a knock-knock joke.

———

Knock, knock.
Who's there?
Gorilla.
Gorilla who?
Gorilla cheese sandwich!

I told you.

Terminals A, B, and C Are Without Power

(Short, Fast, and Deadly, April 2012)

What has happened?

The interrogator's superior was a bureaucrat with a comfortable second layer on his stomach and a mustache. His scuffed, brown shoes were imported from Prague. In 1968.

What has happened?

The bureaucrat had hurried down into the basement after the horrific screaming had suddenly ceased. The orders were for the interrogator not to exterminate the subject.

What has happened?

The interrogator walked around the apparatus and jiggled wires helplessly.

What in Christ's name has happened? Did you kill him?

The interrogator jiggled more wires.

No, sir. Terminals A, B, and C are without power.

Apparatus
(Yareah Magazine, December 2012)

The way the lieutenant spoke of it, one would have thought he was describing a major feat of engineering—something infinitely complex, which carried much import, holding moral and religious high ground, if such things can be lectured upon, or even thought of in the context of a war. It was not a routine briefing. The star was the particular instrument. The few Serbian newsmen standing around smoked Kent cigarettes and constantly picked at invisible specks of lint from their wrinkled suits. It seemed as if they were interested more in the manner in which they smoked, than anything else.

Everyone took great care to distinguish themselves in their technique. They were bored with the war. No one flinched at the close sounds of mortar fire and live charges tearing apart the hills. I scribbled the officer's words in my reporter's notebook with a dull pencil. Cristiano was my photographer. He was from Ravello, a small town on the Amalfi Coast. He was a thin, brown Sorrentian with a fantastic Roman nose who didn't say much, despite his heritage.

"Of course, there will be only one more execution before the apparatus is dismantled," said the lieutenant. "NATO mandate, you see," he excused the fallacy and shook his head melancholically. And then he looked at me for a long time. I was the only American there. It was my fault that the torture and killing mechanism was being put out of commission. For a second I felt guilty.

Cristiano loaded up Tri-X into his camera.

One of the press corps spilled coffee on his own jacket and cursed.

"The parts you see here were all designed by a famous Serb engineer," the officer said. He pointed to the instrument with a pool cue.

"Bratislav Jovanovic. He is a direct descendant of Konstantin Jovanovic who, as you well know, was the architect of our great Parliament building in 1891; the cornerstone of which was laid by King Peter I in 1907."

One of the Serbs pushed a soft pack toward me. I took a cigarette and nodded and he didn't smile or say anything. He smelled of acrid sweat and garlic. The shirt under his arm was wet from perspiration.

"The middle and upper parts are where the pressure is applied. The blades and rotors are driven into the flesh slowly at the kidney, liver, and lung levels, by a pneumatic pump which can also run on a generator, given the present situation with our hydroelectric stations," the lieutenant said. "Usually the confession is extracted within three to five minutes. Our communications officer is videotaping the entire procedure."

"Why?" I asked.

"Everything must be documented in order to ensure the process adheres to military policy standards. In order that the law is not abused," the officer said. He was annoyed with me.

Cristiano affixed the flash.

"In order that the law is not abused?"

"Yes," the lieutenant said. "We have accountability standards in the Serbian Army."

Cristiano twisted on the lens.

"After the information is extracted, the condemned is left on the machine until he perishes. The technician adjusts the setting of the blades and rotors to a lower rate and the convict is given three glasses of Slivovitz in succession as an anesthetic. He has the right to refuse it, although we found that in most cases he is still conscious enough to drink."

The Serb newsmen snickered and elbowed one another, probably at the final fortitude shown by the condemned.

"In our experience, we have found that even the most devout of Muslims drink the alcohol," the lieutenant said. "The machine persuades them to let go of God, even. In that way, it is quite efficient."

The Serbs laughed and dragged on their wrinkled cigarette

butts. The officer looked at the press credentials hanging from my neck.

"You are Romanian, sir?"

"I am American."

"But your last name. Is it not Romanian?"

"It is."

"Ah, see then. We love our brothers next door," the officer said, "despite the Latin alphabet you use. Despite the fact that you're the only ones in the Balkans who've kept the Roman ties."

"Yes, well…we don't have much capacity to retain Glagolitic or Cyrillic," I said. "We get easily confused by *B*s and *R*s and *F*s."

This drew more laughter from the Serb press corps who turned and patted me on the shoulders. More cigarettes were offered.

"In any case," the lieutenant said, "the condemned perishes on the machine within four to six hours from loss of blood. After the execution, the apparatus is scrubbed and disinfected. This is to ensure the elimination of any blood-borne diseases and as protection for the next man scheduled for execution."

No one seemed to acknowledge the irony and futility of that.

Cristiano was ready to shoot.

The officer moved in close to his machine and straightened out his uniform. Then he cleared his throat and smiled.

"A bit more to the right, *tenente*," Cristi said.

Then he hit the shutter and the flash fired. When it was over the Serbs halfheartedly applauded.

Later, in the hotel bar Cristiano said: "Pay close attention to all of this; what is happening here. It is a kind of madness that will not go unnoticed by the West. These pictures will all be used as evidence when these monsters go to trial at The Hague."

I said I didn't believe officers at this level would ever be brought to justice. He said I wasn't a true American. I was too cynical.

"A true American is a humanist. He believes in fairness and justice."

"An idealist, a Pollyanna..."

He said I'd been reading too much Kafka and didn't have faith in the processes of the world.

He was right.

And so was I.

Incident Outside Novi Sad

(FRIGG, October 2012)

The first time I saw a man die I was nine years of age. He died forcefully in a Trabant—a minuscule, boxy, East German car made out of cardboard or something resembling drywall; a car that even we, Romanians, made fun of, although Trabants were quite popular around Bucharest and almost equaled in number the Dacia 1100s that traversed our boulevards and side streets in a weird, self-conscious and paranoid urgency, that of being perpetually watched.

The man, grinding gears and pushing hard a backfiring, oil burning, overheating proletarian motor, was making a run over the border into Yugoslavia. There was no sophisticated plan that I could discern; nothing thought out in advance, no underground tunnel, no homemade hot air balloon envelope sewn from bed sheets like I'd heard in fantastic, successful defection stories from my parents and their friends gossiping at the seaside, covertly listening to Radio Free Europe on their shortwaves and secretly delighting in these shared morsels of attaining freedom in the West.

The man just pointed the front end toward Novi Sad and made a run for it; a simple plan. I don't know where exactly the border was; usually some sort of demarcation like a barrier or concrete parapet would delineate this obtuse, imaginary line two countries historically draw into the land and idiotically defend, so I don't know if he died on Romanian or Yugoslavian soil. I imagine if it were the former, he would have been disappointed, for most of us ordinary citizens are born and die anonymously and uneventfully in the same country—sometimes in the same house, and less often in the same bed. I imagine he would have at least wanted to be able to claim his dramatic demise on foreign soil: mission half accomplished as it were.

The border soldier who shot him from approximately a kilometer away fired his rifle three times before he picked him off with the fourth slug and the hapless, cardboard, Communist machine ground to a feckless halt just short of a tree. Immediately a black, government sedan stopped next to the fallen would-be defector and three men pulled out the body violently and stuffed it into the back seat, one of the agents contemptuously kicking the dead man in between his limp legs in a final act of degradation (or childish revenge).

There was blood on the windshield from where the brain matter splattered. The border soldier had been a good shot. Probably he was going to be commended for his patriotic act; perhaps even given a medal or official papers recognizing his difficult, but honourable feat. And probably, later, like most of the others, he would disappear swiftly into the system: into the salt mines, the gulags, the labour camps, this particular incident long forgotten and officially erased from any resemblance of a record of existence.

My country's history, back then, was dubiously written in pencil. Revision and redaction were highly sought government professions. I was at the drafty window of an acquaintance's summerhouse that year when the running man was killed. I was eating large, round grapes from Ostrov, which my father had brought in the boot of our car in stacked, wooden crates to have as dessert each night. Within five minutes, all evidence of anything having happened had been removed or erased. The border soldier who had taken the shots was picked up by a second black Dacia and driven up the slope toward a small, non descript house made from large granite stones.

Later that evening my parents and their acquaintances played backgammon and drank red, homemade wine and discussed Mircea Eliade. No one spoke of what had happened. If it, indeed, had happened. The lines between several versions of reality were always kept out of focus, whether by the government intending to perpetually destabilize its programmed citizens, or as merely a survival mechanism by familial relations. I understood that well. I was born into that. People lived and died, or didn't live or die at all. And some lived but never died. And others were never born.

The night of the first time I saw a man who was never born, at age nine, I read three chapters of Jules Verne's "Journey to the Center of the Earth." When I finished, I climbed into bed and slept without dreaming.

("Surviving Winter in Copenhagen")
(FRIGG, October 2012)

We relieved ourselves on the left flank of Christiansborg Palace, in plain view of the *Folketinget*, the Supreme Court, Office of the Prime Minister, and—we both hoped—directly below the chambers of Queen Margrethe II. We had travelled from Potsdam to Berlin, two brown boys on a stolen scooter in horizontal rain, then crossed on a ferry at Ahrensoop. Neither of us spoke Danish.

We were hungry and we had no money. So we sat on a kerb in front of the Copenhagen Kommune, across from the National Museum, and begged.

Three consecutive nights we slept on a bench inside Vesterport train station, but eventually we were hustled out by two policemen on bicycles.

A middle-aged prostitute put us up in one room on the promise that we would clean her flat and both bathrooms.

We spent two nights there.

In the daytime we smoked her black hash and ate bread.

There were no jobs for two dark skinned Bulgarian transients.

I spent one afternoon digging out dog shit from the channels cut into my soles.

Anastas picked at a lesion on his cheek.

We had no food that winter in Copenhagen.

Finally, for nine days we were subcontracted by a Chinese family to clean flats and houses.

And then we put up our own fliers in coffeehouses:

hi, we are student of denmark and we are greek and nepal, 22 year old males. we are looking for cleaning job in copenhaven, as we can do good in cleaning. we had cleaned since we was in denmark and we know how to go for it. so, it wil b thankful if u provide us this short of job. we promise to do good in this feild.
thanking you
Prakash Budhathoki and Stavros Costagavras
telefon. 26744075
Rebæk Søpark 5, 6, -748
2650 Hvidore

The telephone number belonged to a public handset in the train station. No one ever called.

~~Anastas prostituted himself to a handful of Japanese businessmen.~~

We smoked Kent cigarettes.

~~And then Anastas~~ ...

The Osseous Tissue of Fish, Two Poems and One Song, How To Safeguard a House Key, They Drank Water Out of Jars, Where The Microphone Is Hidden

(FRIGG, October 2012)

"For you fish, for me sausages."

"But ma."

"I said it only once."

The table had no cover. They ate next to one another staring at the wall.

"Were you a good Pioneer today?"

"Yes ma."

"What did you learn?"

"Two poems and one song. About the revolution."

"Good man. Will you tell them to me after dinner?"

"I'll have to practice still..."

"Good man. When you can. When you're ready."

"Yes ma."

She whispered: "Tonight I'll teach you the Our Father."

"You mean Our Leader?"

"No. Our Father."

"Is it a poem?"

"It's like that. You say it at night, before bed. Before night falls all the way through. Eat your fish."

"It has bones."

"It should."

He spat out tiny, sharp slivers of endoskeleton, which he pushed together into a pile on the side of the plate.

"Uncle Petru drinks yoghurt straight out of the jar."

She laughed.

"...and makes horrible gurgling sounds when he does it."

"Means he likes it."

"It makes me ill."

"Don't exaggerate. Eat more fish."

She slapped him lightly on the back of the head.

"Be nice to Uncle Petru. Without him we'd have no hot water. Or fish."

"But ma."

"Eat. Now. What else?"

"We memorized the periodic table in chemistry."

"Good. What's Lead?"

"Pb."

"Good."

"That's easy. It's just like *plumb*."

"It is. And?"

"Laurentiu pissed on the staircase at yard time. He couldn't hold it any longer."

She sucked something out of her teeth: "Animal. Did they catch him?"

"No."

"Animal."

The boy snickered through his nose.

"Did you remember your key?"

"Yes ma."

"Did you?"

She slapped him lightly on the back of the head again.

"Yes. Ma."

"Where is it now?"

The boy dug into his shirt and brought out the awkward piece of metal, tied to a thin rope hanging around his neck.

"Good man. Eat."

"Tomorrow can I have sausages?"

"Fried potatoes tomorrow."

"Ah, Ma..."

"I said it only once."

They drank out of gigantic, two-liter jars. She had sterilized them with boiling water the night before, while he sat and scrubbed himself in the bathtub. Before they were sterilized, she had pickled cabbage in them. They still tasted like it.

She whispered: "I want you to tell no one about Uncle Petru."

"The yoghurt?"

"Anything about him. Don't even mention him."

"Yes ma."

"Deal?"

"Yes ma."

"Look at me."

"Yes ma. I won't say nothing."

"Good man. Will you recite those poems for me?"

"Yes ma."

"That's my good man."

She said that last bit about the poems much louder. And when she said it, she cocked her head up toward the light fixture in the kitchen. That's where the microphone was.

The Old Ceremony

(Slingshot Litareview, January 2011)

jesus what a big fuss they made over this man who was lying dead shriveling on a table in the middle of the musty parlour. they had stacked make-up on his face, which made him look like a foreshortened monarch or an ogre from a Grimm Brothers' faerie tale. they let the mourners in and immediately two women dressed in black collapsed on the body wailing and weeping and beating with their fists on their own temples.

jesus what a shit of an embarrassing spectacle.

when i go i want you to bury me in a goddamn ditch on the outskirts of the city and be done with it, Marian said. i don't care what happens to me. i don't want any of this.

the women were wailing but eyeing the wine table and moving around the body in their grief closer to the booze and the food.

goddamn moochers, Marian said.

and he went outside and lit a cigarette.

and what do you want on your epitaph i said.

he spat into the dusty road and covered it up with his boot.

he said someone ought to tie fishing gut to one of his wrists and play a fucking practical joke on these mystical grieving zombies. i ever tell you how me and Cezar did that once at a viewing? scared the shit out of the believers when we raised the lady's arm out of the coffin.

he spat again. and laughed. and took a long drag of the Kent, burning it down by a third.

this is shit. all of it. everyone dies like everyone else has ever died. and then they're dead.

Marian was the son of a peasant tractor driver who was assigned to a salt mine when he tried forming a union in the village of Buhusi. Marian spoke English and drank Johnnie Walker stolen from foreigners and tourists who brought the booze in order to bribe border officials and other bureaucrats ensconced into the fabric of the country.

fucking bedbugs, all of them, he said.

i didn't know how to answer that.

let's go back inside. they have feta and tomatoes and bread and
sarmale, he said. let's get it over with.

the body lying in state was his father's. they had found the tractor
driver face down on an embankment by the train tracks. his feet
and hands had been cut off.

The Rubber Penguin
(Necessary Fiction, March 2012)

When I think about Da, that late November morning in the park, I see the horizon line bouncing up and down smoothly and seamlessly. Da and that man called Adam huddled together, standing next to a park bench in black overcoats, rising and falling with the horizon...below the horizon...all of it locked and moving together. The two men resembled magpies. Heckle and Jeckle. That's how I think of Da. My Da. And even though Da was a hard man, especially during that November, I loved him. He was mine. I counted on him for protecting me and helping the two of us through all the strangeness of the autumn and the hard, coming winter.

"Don't swing too high," Da yelled.

Adam, the man who looked like a subservient whisper, turned and raised his hand at me. He smiled with silver teeth, which seemed to absorb the light of the overcast sky.

"Both hands on the chains," Da yelled again, knowing I'd return the friendly gesture.

The horizon rose and fell and the two magpies continued to stand together, each one from time to time stomping out the cold humidity from his bones.

I knew even then who Adam was. There were armies of Adams being educated down in the salt mines. We all knew about the salt mines. We all knew what happened when people disappeared into the earth, down into the quarries to cure whatever respiratory problem they suddenly seemed to have developed. Some we never saw again. Others, like Adam, were let out by the Central Committee; bestowed upon us to reacquaint themselves with us over a small glass of table wine, polenta, and stuffed cabbage leaves; always in the kitchen, and always talking convincingly about something.

Up and down they rose and fell. Da yelled something at me but it got lost in the screeching and huffing of pneumatic bus brakes coming from the boulevard that outlined the patch of trees.

"What?"

I watched Adam, the First Man, take something from his breast, from inside his haggard raincoat, and hand it to Da. It was paper. Its corners were slapped by the wind, and Da tried to keep it from flying off. And he looked at it.

Up and down.

The bus revved up its diesel engine.

And then Da ripped the paper in half, timing the action with the bus roar, which made me smile. He kept both pieces tightly in his hand. The other man, the whisper, lit a cigarette. Da turned and motioned for me to come.

"You're shooting up like a weed," Adam said and opened up his mouth again, ingurgitating whatever light was left in the day.

I shook his hand. He gripped me like the vise the Central Committee had used to shatter the phalanges in his other mitt.

"Too big to be held up by the neck," Da said and the other magpie cackled.

"Remember that?"

"He was three," Da said. "How could he?"

"What's six times nine?"

I told him.

"Now *that's* a Pioneer," Adam said and with his good hand reached into the side pocket of his trench coat and brought up something.

"Miss your mum?"

I told him.

He held out his fist and Da said: "Take it."

"It's all right," Adam said. "Your da said so."

The small, rubber figurine he placed in my hand was clammy and warm, and the white paint was peeling from his distended belly. It was a used toy. It was probably something he had found on the street.

"It's called an Emperor Penguin," Adam said. "Go ahead. It's all right with your da."

"Go ahead."

I shook his hand again.

"You know, in hunting, the Emperor Penguin can remain underwater for eighteen minutes," Adam said.

Da coughed.

"I can do it for ten," he laughed. "Maybe. I know. Not even close. But your da could probably beat that."

And he laughed again. And looked at Da.

"Eight times seven!"

I told him. He placed his hand on my head: "That's a good Pioneer."

After he left, Da and I sat on the bench. He took out a handful of large, purple grapes from the pocket of his overcoat and we ate the fruit in silence in the wind. He spat out the seeds. Grape seeds upset Da's stomach.

"We can have schnitzels tonight," he said. "I can get them at Lido's. With mustard."

"All right."

"You don't have to keep that thing he gave you, you know."

"All right."

There was a large rubbish bin at the exit gate of the park. When we walked by it, Da threw away the torn paper that Adam had given him earlier. I caught a quick look. It was a black and white photograph of a topless woman, smiling, with a bobbed haircut. It looked very much like a young version of my mum.

The Man Who Also Loved Butterflies

How Vladi fell in love with butterflies was: he brought one to his father's cell when he was seven years old. He also brought some fatty chicken broth, which his mother had made for his father, and which his father was allowed to have every ninety days. How Vladi found out what they did to his father was: he simply was allowed to watch through a slit in the iron door. He saw his father on his knees. Standing. It's strange to describe an imprisoned man standing on his knees. Back straight, not leaning on his calves, head and shoulders up. Standing before an incomprehensible force alive just beyond the field of vision the slit allowed. Standing at that force's attention. That's how Vladi saw his father in the cell for three days straight. Nothing more. And though his father was bound by terror, there seemed to be no one else in the iron room alongside him, barking orders or monitoring. For Vladi it seemed like soul cleansing; a sort of meditation the paternal convict was allowed to have. (You should try that and see how you feel after one hour only—back straight now, little Pioneer.)

In his box, many years later, standing at his own interrogator's attention Vladi turned inside deeply and thought of Socrates: "know thyself." And he began: The line dividing good and evil passes through hearts of men, not states, classes, nor political parties. And the line constantly shifts. And as it cuts through the heart of every human being, who is willing to destroy a piece of his own heart? Know thyself, you devil saint.

Confronted by the pit into which he was about to be tossed, Vladi forgot everything. He halted. What he remembered was not actual history, but merely that hackneyed dotted line his interrogator had chosen to drive into his memories by incessant hammering. Earlier, Vladi confessed and signed that throughout his imprisonment he had spent much of his time laboriously dissecting a confusing species of butterflies called Polyommatus blues. He mused on how they had evolved. In his handwritten document he confessed he had lived incarcerated but free with the butterflies. That document was signed in red ink. In it he also betrayed a group of people already executed and buried in mass graves underneath various concrete basements.

The line constantly shifts. Some were lucky enough to have inscriptions on their boxes. *Work fine and you shall be buried in a coffin as well!*

Chunks of Wall
(Yareah Magazine, March 2012)

I still cannot watch Planet of the Apes. The original one with Charlton Heston. In the evenings I would be left alone in the apartment and often times I could not put myself to sleep. I was eight. Some nights I'd panic when it got late and I'd kneel before the large icon of Jesus being held by Mary (it was illegal for us to own religious property, but we did anyway) and pray someone would come home. I am embarrassed to think about that now, but I was a boy and I was just simply scared. I read Jules Verne mostly, and Renart the Fox. I played cowboys and Indians in the park, with sticks, during the day after school. With friends. Boys who grew up to be I don't know. Informers maybe. Traitors. Laborers. Torturers. Prisoners, most likely. Or engineers.

Sometimes I'd be locked out of the apartment until my father would get home hours after I'd get off school, and I'd have to piss badly. Often times I pissed on the stairs of our building, waiting. Waiting. I took some of the nastiest beatings from my father for pissing on the stairs. But I kept doing it. I don't know why. Not even now. I took some of the nastiest beatings also for having terrible handwriting and shitty calligraphy. I wrote in ink and invariably I'd make a mistake and try to cover it up. Scratch out the ink with the corner of a razor blade. It was awful. It was always a botched up job. And my father would wail on me for trying to cover up the mistake. He said he wouldn't be able to correct me if he didn't see the mistake originally. But I kept scratching off the ink. I don't know why I didn't stop. I don't know why I didn't leave the mistake there. I didn't trust him maybe. I didn't trust that he wouldn't beat me anyway. And so I took my chance.

The night of the earthquake I was alone in the apartment and they showed Planet of the Apes on television. The original one. With Charlton Heston. It was on. It was off. And somehow I got myself to sleep before the building started swaying. I got up. It was pitch black. They were there, the two of them. They must have come in. I don't know. It was late. My mother, not realizing

I was out of bed, rushed and picked up an armful of blankets. Or my father. They are the same, my parents. One entity sliced into two halves. Neither one better than the other. Neither one more significant or insignificant than the other. It smelled like chunks of wall. Of paint. Of gas. Of something burning. Like pig's singed hair. Or. Skin. Outside, the building next to ours had half collapsed. There was moaning from the people trapped under concrete and steel. It was foggy. Thick with rubble. A man came out of the dusty cloud and offered to put his hat down so my mother could step into it. We were all barefoot. We slept in the park in which I played cowboys and Indians. No policemen came to tell us to get off the grass. There were no pensioners sitting on benches. There was no sun after that.

I lost a friend in the collapse. A boy. And his mother and father. In the building next to ours. Later, when you looked at it, as it stood untouched and somehow wounded, it seemed a giant sword had sliced down the building vertically. The only thing exposed were the toilets on each floor. I thought it indecent. There were rusty pipes. Toilets and rusty pipes with shit still flowing inside of them. It was an indecent way to be remembered if you lived in one of those units. People were still moaning from underneath the rubble. There were looters. Blankets. Whiskey from the forbidden shops. Kent cigarettes. And days later, German Shepherd rescue dogs with the Red Cross insignia on a white sheet tied around their torsos. People passed judgment on other people. Looters shrugged it all off and found customers who bought the stolen booty. My mother never took the man's hat. Never stood inside of it.

I was sent to the country. To a school there. It was some weeks. Or months. Time flows strangely for an eight year old. I had English class and I said things like: "yellow." Or: "this is the house that Jack built." Or: "an egg in an egg cup." I bathed in a large bucket with water that had been heated by my grandma on the stove. I took the first shift, the cleanest water, before my grandpa got in and had his wash. My father sent a letter that said structural engineers were reinforcing our apartment building and that I'd be able to return shortly. Meanwhile there was: "advertisement" and "good night" and "I am well, and how are you?" in English class. I learned how to build a raft from saw grass or corn stalks or reeds from the other boys in the village. Once, by accident, I struck one of them in the head with a large tree branch I had found in the fields, and was swinging above my head like a lasso. I was sent back I don't know when. Time flows in weird patterns for an eight year old.

It hardly rains in the summer in this city. Later, I am to find out it's on the same latitude as Montreal and that explains the brutal winters. It doesn't look anything like Montreal, though. Later I find that out, as well. The boulevard, ten stories below, is soaked with whipping gusts of water. It's deserted. The boulevard is most always deserted. The half-standing apartment building next to ours is getting a new half. Walls are being raised around the exposed toilets, up on each floor. It's like someone is slowly covering the flesh of a bashful, discreet, abused child standing in the middle of a cold, interrogation room. There are laborers hammering steel into concrete. Raising parapets looks violent and wrong and not at all elegant. Our apartment buildings are all institutional and remind me of dormitories or hospitals. I watch the workers out of our kitchen window, which has thin chicken wire attached and rigged by my father just outside the glass— puffed out in a weird way—in order to prevent me from falling out if the window is opened. One man is on a higher floor peering down below in the torrential rain. He yells:

"Costa!"

No one answers except the persistent rain hitting the glass of our kitchen window.

"Costa!"

The floor of the kitchen moans and I know my father has entered the room.

"Costa!"

The laborer is peering down seven stories. He stands on a wide open sheet of concrete, close to the edge, and I know if he leans out much further he'll come down fleshy and soft and spongy.

"Costa!"

The kitchen floor moans again and my father asks something about eating take-away schnitzels from the pub near Lido's, for dinner.

"Costa!"

Rain. Chunks of wet concrete. "Yellow." My father: "...and potatoes?" This is the house that Jack is building. "It's not AD-ver-tisements, it's ad-VUHR-tisments. You are learning the Queen's English."

"Costa!"

"What?"

The first laborer leans over further and yells:

"Fuck your mother up the ass!"

And then he laughs and flicks his cigarette butt over the open platform, down to the wet ground.

The Prune Eaters
(BRICKrhetoric, February 2012)

The ones with the bad suits, the young ones that had yellow teeth and hastily arranged hairdos with sticky saliva, were informers. They were caretakers with small notebooks in their breast pockets. They stood in front of buildings, in piazzas, in parks, in train stations, in front of university student housing.

Their suits were ill-fitting; some hung loose and low and were wrinkled by weather and yellowed by the acrid odor of the summer underarm. Others were tight, exploding on them like thin scarves wrapped around bulbous melons and held together feebly with string.

Within every territory or section that these men watched they knew where the prune trees were. They were young men with old faces. They were all peasants with notebooks arrived from the countryside on trains. In sour smelling compartments.

They were trained to spot people that looked like philosophers or writers. Or that looked like they were deep in thought. Or that were capable of thought. They were trained to write down descriptions and routes; mannerisms and intentions.

And at the end of their shifts, the informers went out of their way to walk by the prune trees. The branches hung low. Supervisors stuffed their attachés with green, unripe prunes. They worked quickly. They stuffed their pockets. Their satchels. Sacks. They picked only once and hoped to eat many times from the bounty. Anything more would have looked suspicious.

When the pockets stretched out, swollen with green fruit, they would walk away quickly. Because *prune eater* was synonymous with *excrement eater*. Because a prune eater was the lowest, most unscrupulous animal and deserved to be sent to the salt mines or gulags just for that alone.

But the green prunes drove them insane. They took them away from their duties. They brought back their old habits, in the villages, of stealing from neighbors' trees. They weren't hungry for green prunes. They were hungry for the sour taste of poverty that took them back to their childhood beds.

I watched them stuff their satchels, the froth on their teeth giving away their transgressions. They ate quickly while walking and to myself I said: you are not allowed to eat the green fruit. The pit is still soft. You are eating pieces of Death.

Vanya
(Guernica, May 2012)

Uncle Miki wasn't my real uncle but ever since I could remember he was called Uncle Miki. And so. That spring the war still moved north but we did not go to it any longer. Uncle Miki took me away from the city one night with his sputtering Trabant. You want to play 007? he said. You know 007, yes? I answered. Keep quiet then, and stay low. I didn't understand; it was pitch black and no one could see inside the tight cabin. Uncle Miki drove the little car with the hole in the floor with nervous urgency. During the getaway, I pretended we were in Fred Flintstone's car and in order to stop, we'd have to shove our feet down the hole in the floor and onto the pavement. On the way we saw an overturned buggy with a dead horse. The wind was strong enough to spin the upturned wooden wheel.

We were given a room in the back of a peasant's house in a village by the seaside. The room backed to the outhouse. Initially, Uncle Miki protested to me only, which I didn't understand. There was nothing I could do about any of it. But the outhouse, strangely, didn't smell. There were pictures on the wall of a funeral and of an open casket with mourners standing all around. The deceased was a boy about my age. He wore a suit with a tie and a gladiola had been placed on his chest, just above his intertwined hands. Framed on another wall was a letter in pristine calligraphy. It's Russian, Uncle Miki said, squinting at the Cyrillic letters. *Vanya piereti mierti ubit masinoi.* Everything in that room was written in Russian. Uncle Miki said the boy's name was Vanya and that he had been run over by a fuel truck just in front of this house. I think the peasant is the boy's father, Uncle Miki said as he pulled out nose hairs with his fingernails while looking in the mirror. When he said that, he didn't move his lips. It's weird living in a room with a dead boy all over the walls, I said. Uncle Miki laughed. What does it matter? He's dead. You don't believe in ghosts, do you?

In the summer, Uncle Miki taught me how to play backgammon. And the peasant's wife made cow's tongue for us every Friday evening. One day Uncle Miki told me that there was no Saint Nicholas and that it was grownups that left candies and gifts inside your boots at night, while you were sleeping. He also said that sheep weren't really fallen clouds. That night I dreamed that donkeys pulling peasants' carts could parallel park in the city.

In the fall, Uncle Miki told me I'd have to move away from the country. He told me I was a Jew and that he'd arranged to have me taken on a Turkish cargo ship waiting in the Adriatic, to Izmir. What does it matter that I'm a Jew, I asked him. They're killing Muslims. Why do I have to be taken to another country? And he said Jews were a bonus. They've always killed Jews, he said. And they'll always kill them.

The night we left Vanya to his own room again, the house dog—a German shepherd—had gotten loose from his chain. The peasant and his wife went out into the street whistling, and Uncle Miki shushed them while he tried to start the Trabant from third gear. Come push along with me, he whispered, and I helped slowly roll the car forward from the passenger side. The peasant disappeared into his kitchen and came out with two knives, which he rubbed together instead of whistling. He always comes to this, he said and winked at us as we struggled. He thinks he's getting meat for dinner, the rascal.

I looked back through the dirty glass while Uncle Miki grinded the gears and cursed and spat out the window. We were moving fast and it didn't make any sense to me why he was so mad. For a moment, as we left the peasant's house buried in the darkness, I thought I saw the dog run after our car. This bloody fucking century Uncle Miki said . . . began and ended in Yugoslavia.

But it wasn't the German shepherd. It wasn't a dog at all.

De Aardappeleters
(Connotation Press, January 2012)

Brother breathed within everyone. The poor were easy. He got them with potatoes. The rest welcomed Him early in the morning, roused out of bed—puzzled and disoriented—and usually embraced Him soon enough in a police station basement or minuscule torture cell, usually nursing excruciating wounds to their genitals, spinal chords, teeth, or anal canals; all the while looking for pieces of their pulled fingernails to cover up the rapidly infecting raw flesh and ooze dripping from the top of their broken digits. Brother didn't need to hold up any fingers and ask test questions. He burrowed inside hearts and minds and travelled through short waves nightly to generations of transistors across heavily fortified borders.

But the poor were easy. All they needed to be turned was the tuberous, starchy perennial waving under their nose. Brother's fingers didn't bury the potatoes in the earth; the poor would search there first—it was logical. They were peasants. Brother didn't like the peasants' relationship with the soil; it was too intimate. The layers of Terra would harbor too many secrets, too many cherished ideas, which it would never spit back, no matter how much Brother abused and scorched it. He hid the potatoes in cities so the poor would flock to Him where there was no soil, just paved, wide boulevards and statues with proclamations of truncated history and fictitious battle victories. Brother said humanity really only began with the Revolution of His birth fifty years back. How many fingers is He holding up?

Gabby first saw the dirty spud rolling across a muddy lot on the outskirts of the city, just across from gypsy encampments. There had been a government housing compound standing there, but the 7.2 that flattened the capital in Spring had brought most of it down, and all that remained was an obtuse skeleton made from concrete and steel rods, exposing a five-story wing of toilets and sinks. It was as if some giant ogre sliced down the middle of the building with his sword, leaving behind only a choleric fossil of people's deepest intimacies: their porcelain commodes, the sponges with which they cleaned their private areas, their toothbrushes.

Gabby followed the potato around the ruins and through what was a courtyard used for hanging rugs on parallel steel bars, and beating the dust and mites out with bamboo paddles. The spud turned through mud and straw and Gabby chased it and worried all the while. Three Arabs in a Trabant drove by and one man spit out the window at Gabby and called him a gypsy. They all smoked hand rolled cigarettes and held contraband in the form of Kent cigarettes and Johnnie Walker Black in the car's anemic boot. The machine backfired and blended into the Arabs' roars of laughter and weird, cursing language.

Now onto Revolution Boulevard and across it and through abandoned farmers' markets and circling a piazza that once held a bronze statue of Romulus and Remus suckling at the Mother Wolf's teats. Brother's fingers were nimble and He played with Gabby as He played his tailor made games with everyone else. Of the things Brother excelled at the most, was rolling potatoes away from the poor. Like the Tri-Colored Piper of Hameln. (Red out!)

Now down alleys soaking in school children's piss and shit, now hopping on and off the concrete steps of the Athenaeum, now around the base of the Infinite Column, while Gabby pursued it with his hands in his trouser pockets. It took him to the door of a well known television producer or personality or director, Gabby wasn't sure. It was the most beautiful door Gabby had ever seen. Wood. Brass. Gold. Silver. Something else. Gabby wanted to knock at it. He wanted to see the man come out. He had never seen a television man before. Would he wear a terrycloth robe? An ascot? Would he have a nice haircut? Would he use a Water-Pik for his teeth? But Brother rolled the potato. It traversed asphalt streets pockmarked by sinkholes, gravel roads, and well-travelled bus routes. It hopped rides in empty bags carried by weathered pedestrians looking to line up for something to eat and bring it home. And Gabby followed it everywhere.

Hands in pockets. Furrowed brows with worry.

"Filthy gypsy," one of the boys said and hit Gabby across the bridge of his nose. Gabby heard a snap and felt the blood flood the olfactory canals and rush out onto his shirt.

"Beat him with the fucking potato," someone said, and they struck Gabby in the temples, in his forehead, on his jaw.

"Here, here's your dinner, you filthy gypsy."

"You lousy dog. You thief."

They forced the dirty spud into Gabby's mouth and Gabby thought they were going to suffocate him. In his bloody state he eyed a stage curtain slowly drawn up to reveal the glorious statue of Romulus and Remus with the She-Wolf.

They left him sitting in the gravel, a bag of broken bones, and as they headed out, the big one—the one with the lisp—took a vicious boot to Gabby's ribs.

"At's a helluva penalty kick you fuckin' imbecile," one of them said, and they roared grossly and thickly, like overburdened mules with whooping cough.

Gabby pushed out the potato with his bloody tongue. It fell in between his legs and wobbled a bit before it settled in a pool of mucus, spit, and blood.

"Move your ass," a driver yelled at a lady crossing the boulevard with a burlap sack filled with potatoes, draped onto her shoulders. And then he honked.

The Sun Eaters
(The Monarch Review, February 2012)

We ran together on the frozen mother land like a pack of disoriented hyenas. Children. Boys, mostly. All ages. Starving. Shit-poor. Ill-dressed. Some dying from tuberculosis or dysentery. Others living with pneumonia, coughing up liquefied guts and bile and epochs of cruelty and the violence our fathers bestowed upon us with belts, shovel handles, tree limbs, chains. We puffed on used, dry butts we found in the rubble of the war. Shit, Russian or Romanian, half smoked, hastily rolled cigarettes; some abandoned by their owners in a hurry, running into the trenches away from whistling mortars, others interrupted by a sudden, violent end. All tainted by once-infected lips. Herpes. Blisters. Cankers. Split lips. Remnants discarded by the dead. Faint footprints. We made up games and stories, all the while subsisting in the shadows of destruction, vagabond concrete, and petrified bones:

"Enemy sniper dragged his last breath on this just before he was clipped by his counterpart."

"He was shot through his own scope."

"On the last day of the war."

"Before he was to come back to his wife."

"And then he was eaten by feral dogs."

"By feral cats."

"By hungry villagers, hiding in their cellars."

"By us."

There was no food (we found 120 grams of bread under a fallen oak tree once), just the winter earth under our thin, worn out soles. (Our thin, worn out souls.) Some had no shoes at all. Others improvised. Gabriel wrapped his feet in gauze. It was soaked in dried blood that looked more like cracked, satiated clay. He had removed the bandage from the frozen head of a captain, propped up against a tree in the forest, on the outskirts of the city. He had removed the captain's stripes, as well, and ate them.

"He died heroically after fighting at Stalingrad."

"There was a sign nailed to his chest that warned of resistance."

"They tortured him but he gave away nothing."

"On the last day of the war."

"Before he was to come back to his wife."

We starved and became insane. We ran together and apart and together again. There was no food. Just cold. Gabriel lost a toe to frostbite. We slid on ice on the bare flesh of our baby feet. We shat in abandoned outhouses. In February, Caesar found a bombed communication truck in the middle of a ravine, hidden by a pyramid of burned out tree trunks. Three men were frozen inside at the controls. Parts of their flesh were black, missing, a leathery-smooth nightmare. It looked like they were smiling, only we knew...it was the grimace of pain and death in that unavoidable instance you cross the bleeding fields or wherever in hell your religion tells you you're going.

"All made from wax by Madame Tussauds."

"Keepers of the Chamber of Horrors."

"You idiots, check their pockets for cigarettes."

"Imbecile!"

"Animal."

"Sodomite."

And in the end, when there was nothing left and we had all come to look like whispers, we ate the sun. It was Pavel who taught us. It was he who convinced us that we'd fill up our bellies with it. There was nothing to eat anymore, and when you have nothing, you will believe anything. Even Pavel with his provincial tales. And so he showed us how to find the few sunny spots, kneel down, turn our faces up to the star, and open our mouths. That was all we had. And so we ate sun. And our mouths became dry and burnt and full.

And that is how we died, one by one.

Breadcrumbs
(Blue Fifth Review, March 2012)

They left the boy in the musty, rancid parlor, alone, with the thing lying in the casket. The boy sat on a chair with a foreshortened leg, at the far corner. The chair teeter-tottered on the wooden floor, making a clicking noise which bounced off the yellow walls and back into the boy's ears. It sounded like slats of wood being flung against concrete. He reached into his pocket and squeezed the little rubber penguin toy his father's friend had given him in the park a few days before. Outside the room they were fighting over who would get the house, the land, the chess set, the broken violin, the Leica, the pictures, the animals, even the chemical trays the old man had used to develop photos in his homemade darkroom, which no one would use anyway.

The boy was angry. Boiling at the strange, leather faced women who had come to the viewing and had broken down on their knees, wailing and beating the casket with their fists, making a familiar, requisite spectacle in the name of charity wine and *coliva*. The soul of the reposed person is only as good as the *coliva* prepared in his memory. That's what the priest had said. The boy fumed. He hated *coliva*. It was just some lousy boiled oats and powdered sugar. No one's life ought to be measured by that. He hated the show. The spectacle of the after-death was sickening. The *Parastas* was to follow before the burial and the same veiled women would be there, again beating on the casket with grief stricken fists; again sucking down red wine and filling up on charity lunch—stuffed grape leaves and sausages. They would place small icons in the coffin, with a hand cross and even a prayer rope in the palms of the deceased.

"O, pray before the Christian who has reposed before the Lord!"

This was no longer his grandfather, this…dead thing. Just some quick hardening matter lying on display like an animal in a taxidermy shop.

A shrunken head, neatly shaved. Macabre make-up and rouge. Small, pursed lips.

The last day of summer, before they cut off the boy's hair to go to first grade and sent him back to the city, the old man snapped photos of him swinging a wooden tennis racquet, in a quick succession of shots. There were about twenty in all, black and white, made with the Leica. Those were his favorite. He pretended he was Nastase playing Connors. He had long, dirty blonde hair and his front tooth had fallen out the night before, but in the photos he was smiling and swinging a forehand at an invisible yellow ball: a massive groundstroke straight out of the fifth set on the lawns of Wimbledon. There were also photos of the day after, taken by his father: the schoolboy with obtusely chopped hair and a checkered white and blue shirt—the red, pioneer cravat tied neatly around his neck. Such a good, young communist. He looked like a defeated zek. Like those people coming out of the salt mines after years of interrogation. The day before and the day after. That's the line you cross. That's how fast it comes. There is nothing tangible for the living or the dead save pomp and circumstance. Tradition. And the things people leave to be remembered, the important things…footprints, smudges on glass windows, written papers, paintings…they're cleaned up and sterilized and packaged for the wake. They're erased to make room for wailing mourners and sweet, boiled, charity oats. Professional funeral crashers.

A heavyset woman came into the parlor swinging the doors violently. She startled the boy who was thinking about smoking a cigarette he had stolen from his uncle earlier. He'd been seven when he first inhaled the stale smoke of a Marasesti hand rolled cigarette, and he'd tried covering up his breath by chewing mint leaves which grew wild in the fields behind his grandfather's house. The woman came in with a white cloth and began to wipe down the tables. Everything went on the floor.

"Eh. What are you still doing here?"

She didn't look up at him, she just wiped and shook out the cloth automatically, not glancing at the shrinking body in the casket at the front of the parlor.

"Eh? Go already you little moocher."

Everything went on the floor. Napkins too.

Everything.

She stepped around the tables, crushing the breadcrumbs under her shoes. They crackled like fragile bones under a car compactor.

"Go on now," she said and blew her nose into the same cloth with which she was cleaning.

"There's another one coming later this afternoon and this place has to be spic and span."

Two Sides of One Half
(Connotation Press, January 2012)

Elvis is dead.

I found out about Elvis queued at a railroad crossing, standing behind a rusted barrier, waiting for the CFR locomotive to pass, pulling cars filled with coal and granite.

August 1977?

Only, when I found out it had taken a month for the news to travel across the water and into the Balkans. Elvis didn't mean shit to me. Never has and never will.

There was gravity in the news as I remember it but all I did was watch the monasteries go by the window of the little Fiat my uncle drove across Transylvania.

"The Magyars hate us, boy."

"And the Japanese?"

He laughed.

I didn't like my uncle. He made awful noises when he slurped yoghurt.

I was in his care that summer. He had a chattering telex in his flat, in the hallway by the bathroom. He was a newspaperman who wrote flowery reportage and sometimes covered Handball and Football.

The Magyars hate us.

So what. I didn't much care for any of that nonsense. Everyone hated someone. We hated the Jews. They hated the Lebanese. We hated the Soviets and the homosexuals.

"Don't forget the gypsies."

And the gypsies.

Everyone hated someone.

I hated Trabants made in East Germany.

The previous spring my father attempted to pass a car and miscalculated the distance of oncoming traffic. He steered into a ditch and split the frame around a strong oak, which didn't give. I was entrusted in my uncle's care that summer while my parents recovered.

Therapy was driving around the countryside with a little Grundig cassette player in the back seat and a handful of Glen Campbell tapes.

"Elvis is dead, boy. You hear me?"

I did. But blamed the locomotive noise rumbling by us at the railroad crossing. I pointed to my ears. I didn't give a shit about Elvis. He was a concept. He didn't belong in my life. Neither did the Magyars or the clergy who often put us up for the night in the monasteries.

The telex ran day and night.

"Do the Japanese hate us, uncle?"

"Shut it."

Like a Rhinestone Cowboy

Riding out on a horse in a star-spangled rodeo

Like a rhinestone cowboy

Getting cards and letters from people I don't even know

And offers comin' over the phone

There was also Boney M. and, of course, Elvis. I didn't listen to any of it. I just watched the country rushing by the back window of the Fiat. And the cracked road roaring under my feet through the rusty hole in the bottom of the car.

"Keep your legs up, boy. Don't let them fall through."

He laughed.

And shook his head: "...do the Japanese hate us...Jesus, this kid."

May Day
(PANK, May 2011)

I chipped my bottom front tooth wrestling with Codrut in his fancy flat in the center of the city. Codrut was the son of a secret police officer who was not so secret and who was not an officer (he was an interrogator; a genius at pulling out fingernails with needle nose pliers). In the days that we found out we were going to be let to emigrate, Codrut—my best friend and my best tooth chipper—stopped talking to me. Despite that, I gave him my skateboard, which was bought by my mother from the Sears catalogue the previous summer. The skateboard was before my mother disappeared in Detroit and never came back with the promised sweets and candies and Buster Brown shoes I was looking forward to wearing and parading before all the fellows at recess. The toys and the clothes were before that too.

After arriving in Detroit, I wrote letters to all the fellows I had known since first grade. No one responded. And I understood why. The secret police would request meetings with their parents if they wrote back. The secret police would probably request meetings anyway. This is what happened, then, to all the ones you left behind. They all had to somehow defend themselves from the acts of treason you committed.

Years later, maybe in 1993, I received a letter from Codrut. He had taken part in the demonstrations against the Party the December the Iron Curtain finally fell. He had been shot in the spine by an army officer and was now riding in a wheelchair made in Germany. He was an engineer working for Renault and was going to be in Detroit for a conference on aerodynamics and design. And would I meet him for a few drinks at Bookies Bar and Grille on Cass Avenue if I had the time and if I could forgive him for banishing me after I'd left. Surely I understood the immense pressure he and his family came under after I emigrated.

The first thing I ever saw on colour television in the States was Battlestar Gallactica. I didn't understand why, from time to time, it would end, and commercials would come on. My first friend in America was Mike Gaydos. After a few months, I got in with some other fellows who started teasing me for being friends with someone named GAYdos. And so, to fall in line with the others, I began to ostracize him as well. Mike eventually moved to Virginia Beach, after we beat him up mercilessly one winter afternoon before class. Because of his last name. They called him a faggot. And I kicked him, along with all of them. So I could fit in.

The Barber
(A-Minor Magazine, July 2012)

Same?

The man in the chair grunts.

And the sideburns? Same tight line?

The man grunts again.

The barber works around the back of the neck meticulously, using short strokes and wiping the white paste from the blade on a small hand towel he keeps draped across his left shoulder. He does a slow, semicircle shuffle around the man's back looking probing judging. Then scraping quickly with the sharp edge.

Family? All right?

The man grunts, but gentler, and shrugs.

The barber says Nah, and pushes down on his customer's shoulders.

Coming around to the throat.

The barber lifts slowly under the chin. The man acknowledges with a Mhm. His Adam's apple pops up. The barber withdraws the blade and lets the laryngeal prominence fall back down before he gets back to work.

You know in the Old West a customer used to hold a pistol to the barber's ribs when he had his throat shaved.

Mhm.

The Adam's apple pops back up again.

Nah. Only I talk.

…

Guess nobody trusted nobody back then. The barber controls his snicker by pushing air through his nostrils, holding his blade very still on the man's flesh.

…

When he's done, the barber wipes off the man's face with a hot towel. Splashes something on his hands. Grabs the man's face and pats. He reaches around the neck, unfastens the white sheet, and shakes off excess hair. Then he sweeps up around the chair, picks up the clippings and hands them to the man, who puts them in a plastic box.

All right?

All right.

The man wipes off his shoulders, opens the door, the bell rings, and he steps through and out.

What was all that abou'?

The other man waiting for his turn.

All what?

The hair in the box thing? What was that?

It's what he wants after every haircut.

Strange.

The barber says: he uses it for his dolls. He makes dolls for the village kids. He used to make them in the concentration camp. Before. You know. Before.

Pawning Dowry
(Necessary Fiction, November 2012)

My name is Ashish but I do not tell them that. It sounds too much like the thing you smoke, and so I call myself Ash. I am a Pakistani, but I do not tell them that either. They mostly think I am Indian. I am brown. So that is what they think. When they ask if I am from India, I nod and smile. It is not a good thing right now to tell white people that you are from Pakistan. And they cannot distinguish between a Paki or a West Bengali English accent, so when they ask, I begin to tell them the fictitious story of my life as an orphan, spent in Calcutta in the care of an uncle who repaired shoes in a little kiosk by the Ganges River Delta. I usually lose them by this point. White people here are not really interested in anything that does not directly affect or involve them. Somehow, though, they care more about Indians than they do about Pakistanis. So I lie.

My real country, Pakistan, means "Land of the Pure" in Urdu, Sindhi, and Persian. It is the sixth most populous country in the world. I am a Muslim. It is not good to be a Muslim right now, if you live among white, Christian people. People here like Hindus. Buddhists, too. So I lie. I went to Quad-i-Azam University in Islamabad and studied biological sciences with Doctor Samina Jalali. My father was a Pashtun and my mother was a Punjabi. Did you know we have glaciers? K2 and Nanga Parbat are in my country. These are mountains over 26,000 feet high. We have deserts, too. The Thar Desert is in the east, and the Tharparkar in the southern province of Sindh is the only fertile desert in the world.

I came to the United States in 2004 on a student visa. I obtained a SAIS Fellowship in Biology to the Johns Hopkins University in Baltimore. I came with my wife, Saira, and we lived for one year in Greenbelt, Maryland. During that time, Saira worked as a teacher's assistant at a daycare center in one of the worst areas in the United States. We had one car, which I took to school, and Saira was left to walk two miles each way to work. She was robbed at gunpoint three times during that year. The third time, it was by a gang of young children in middle school. They beat her with the handle of the gun, and she became permanently deaf in her left ear. After that she begged me to pack and go home, but I had two more years left on the Fellowship and I refused to leave. We had many fights and each time she would turn her head to the side to hear better, and my heart hurt to see her do that, but still I refused to leave. I was a stubborn man. I took a job at nights as an orderly at Doctors' Hospital, not very far from our apartment. With the extra money we were able to buy a small car for Saira to take to work. It was a 1972 orange Toyota Corolla. It had holes in the floor, from the rust, and Saira joked that it looked like a Fred Flintstone car. It was a standard transmission. I taught Saira how to drive it in one Saturday. She was a fast learner, and by midafternoon we were going down Cipriano Road at sixty-five miles per hour, Saira driving and screaming and laughing. We had rolled down the windows and her long hair was being whipped around her face and I called her Medusa. She joked that I was beginning to talk like the Americans. But I told her she was wrong, and that not many Americans know that Medusa is Greek Mythology. Not many Americans know that there were three of them, the Gorgon sisters. And Saira drove like a madwoman the little orange Flintstones car with holes in the floor, and screamed and laughed that she could now drive standard, like a man. Just then, I loved her with her hair like that. More than ever. She was happy. It was the only time I saw her happy here.

In the summer I had a premonition driving on my way to University. I was waiting at a red light on North Charles Street and everything stopped. People and cars and even the clouds stopped from moving. Then, a young, brown woman in a maroon silk *Lehnga* crossed in front of me. She turned and looked into my eyes through the glass, and transformed herself into a dove from the *Panchatantra*. Before she could fly away, a bullet ripped through her white chest and tore apart everything. All insides were on the outside suddenly, in an explosion of flesh and bone and feathers.

Saira was killed in a car accident that day. A man from Clinton, Maryland drove a big truck through a red light at an intersection in New Carrollton and hit the Flintstones car on the driver's side. The man lived. He was not even hurt. Saira was coming back from work. The police said when they pulled her out, there was an indentation of the Toyota insignia from the steering wheel, into her side, where the ribs were broken.

I did not finish my studies at Johns Hopkins. In the following months I took Saira's dowry, piece by piece, to a pawnshop on Riverdale Road not far from the apartment in which I now live, to pay the rent and buy food. I work during the day now at a dry cleaner owned by an Indian family. I work at the front counter with the sixteen-year-old son called Mehu who smokes many cigarettes in the back, and chews gum. He is a mute. On Friday and Saturday nights I work as a busboy at a restaurant called The Silver Quill in Hyattsville, Maryland. It is a bad restaurant.

I have never wanted to go back to Pakistan despite everything that has happened, and despite the fact that it is my home country.

A Well-Trained Horse Can Sometimes Say I Love You

(Subtle Fiction, June 2012)

After they took him down the Quartermaster had his men roll over a cart with various implements used in the butchering of animals.

You know Quartermaster is a non-commissioned rank in many navies he said with droopy eyes and he sharpened the blade against a straight razor horne.

The men had gathered around the twitching animal and were watching their superior methodically working on the sharp edge.

There's no need to use a leather strop the Quartermaster declared as he tested his work with one of his own hairs.

He lowered the follicle onto the blade at a perpendicular angle and the hair gave easily splitting without a sound.

What will you do with a straight razor sir one of the men asked this animal may not give in to such a small blade.

The Quartermaster moved to the head of the fallen beast and sliced out its eye, which ran down into his hand like a poached egg.

And so now the Quartermaster said,

we're ready.

Nathaniel Thurhurst
(Atticus Review, April 2012)

Book One: To The Lighthouse

Sometimes, at night, the wolf is at the door of the gallery.

In the beginning, after the end, I looked up at stars and blocked out the street lamps with my right hand. I never learned where the big dipper or Ursa Major was. I don't see it, even now, through squinted eyes and the smallest hole I make with my index finger and thumb.

No one is spared at night.

She thinks this: "the love it takes to become a man." She thinks this from her chamber, in the beginning, after the end. She will name her child Benjy. I know he is named after the brother of Joseph in the book of Genesis. Benjamin.

I think this: "the love it takes to destroy a man."

And the secret that I know will be buried with me when they fit me into the wooden box like a piece of a jigsaw. When I was twelve I ripped out the hands of the family clock. I thought I could stop time. This thing that seemed to flow to everyone else but me. This made up thing. I wanted it to stop from going forward. I wanted it to run backwards so I could erase what I saw in that room between my brother and my sister. He is Laertes and she is Ophelia in a consanguineous marriage. Genesis was torn up with extreme prejudice by a pauper's calloused hands.

Book Two: As The Stars Fall

A man is the sum of his misfortunes. One day misfortune will get tired and leave, and then time becomes his misfortune. But time is dead as long as it's being counted by little wheels. Only when the clock stops does time come to life.

Ophelia.

and Laertes.

Diminishing without progress.

For me, the line of this history is broken up in pieces of time and scrambled. Ophelia and Laertes. Time has laid hold of a frozen speed. Time is that which separates. We can no longer enter into our past loves and so we find anguish. It's not when you realize that nothing can help you—religion, pride, love, sorrow, anything. It's when you realize you don't need any aid. And then the stars will fall.

Dulce et Decorum Est
(Marco Polo Arts Magazine, May 2012)

Channeling poets in the middle of the night and...

Three shoes on a piano. I find. Three shoes on a piano. And an ashtray full of soot. To-day I woke up to war and the soothing sounds of wooden wind chimes. I read Wilfred Owen from a dug up trench in the middle of stalemate, with a rotting body under me and a cup of steaming tea, balancing on the dead man's boot. Rats carried the plague, handing batons in a savage game of relay. Oswestry in Shropshire. Somehow, Owen channeled Siegfried Sassoon and Rupert Brooke and I fought with these men under the dim light of a fifteen-watt bulb beneath the frozen earth. Three weeks before the Armistice. I fought out with them the meaning of war and patriotism. Or, rather, the meaningless energy of war and patriotism. War within war. War all the time. "How do you explain phosgene? Or mustard gas? Chlorine? Chloropicrin? Lewisite?" In my dream, Owen takes me to Sambre-Oise canal, where he was killed in action in November, 1918. I don't know it's a dream. There are no indications of fluctuating light levels, but neither do I reach for switches in hopes of cutting off electricity. My dreams are just as real as my waking life. In my dreams I often die.

"And then what happens?"

Nothing.

It's as if I switch off a light. Everything goes black. There is nothing bright. There doesn't seem to be a god. Just darkness.

Which brings me back to varying light levels.

In my dream, the bullet enters through the sternum and the lights go off.

This negates the dream state and underscore reality.

Light levels. Fluctuating.

In reality, I am not alive. There seems to be no time passing either forward or backwards. We are lemons.

We are chairs in an Ionesco play.

Ants on a rotating system governed by elemental laws of physics.

We are: oxygen, carbon, hydrogen, nitrogen, calcium, and phosphorus.

Mere elements.

Ars Poetica *co-written with Helen Vitoria*
(Firestorm Literary and Arts Journal, September 2012)

I know about what hangs around tomorrow:
        fire, fasting, spit shine of furniture, a body hinged &
muzzled, hooves

Medusa with a pail of poisoned water & a cup, with rabid teeth
        fever & succubae; nixies sliding down discreetly on well-
oiled, silky cobwebs
        whispering sweet while sharpening her knives

sacrament of blades, slick & sleek, bare contours of bores, bits &
pistons
        like water holding the frequency of winter or ink fevered

This is the season come back 'round for heavy lifting
        & her, sawing through my bones; discontent of piety

I am a dwarf, walking with rusty hammer & dull sickle
        weight of centuries, villages, fields & ploughshares
        pushes down hard & strains my back; looking for lost,
calm animals

But, the animals. Silent. Calm. Scattering in water & light
        pushing through hunger, saying: *this is the future, we sink in
its sound*
        They sing a cryptic language I don't understand

I am, it is my folly, and before them, bone by bone, I petrify
        don't turn, don't stare, whisper the beasts

I am trudging through a canvas sack of iron bearings slung about
my shoulder
        I am all nervous system & insomnia

A structure of envelopes & sun,   burning—

small bits of soul, breath, bile, and arsenic packed hastily
into the sealed patina, a time capsule of leftovers; stale
breadcrumbs for historians to rehydrate & put together
an unknown life in some specific time

                                        until she
                               returns as shelter

Digits

12345

Joyce never worked for me. none of it.
(nunavut.)
not Portrait not Dubliners, Ulysses,
nor Finnegan's.
should
've
if you think about it.
based on labels: **modernism**
ima
gism
instead
what fascinated me about
James
Augustine
Aloysius
were his gargantuan hands
and elongated fingers.
all i can think of when i hear Joyce mentioned in conversations
is the dexterity he must have had on the Underwood
as he was banging out the words.
Thelonius Monk and Vladimir Horowitz
hold the same obtuse fascination.
as do Scott Joplin and Fats Waller.
those oblong digits
working their magic on keyskeyboardstimelinesofhistory.
they save us.

---

they save us.
(line missing)
working their magic on keyskeyboardstimelinesofhistory.
those oblong digits
as do scott joplin and fats waller.
hold the same fascination for me.
thelonius monk and vladimir horowitz

joyce never worked for me. none of it.

(unavut.)

not portrait not dubliners, ulysses,

nor finnegan's,

should

ve,

if you think about it.

based on labels: **modernism**

ima

gism

what fascinated me about

james

augustine

aloysius

were his gargantuan hands

and elongated fingers.

all i can think of when i hear joyce

is the dexterity he must have had on the underwood

as he was banging out the words.

Grab It The Bucket
(Bizarro Central, March 2012)

You pair tiramisu with a crayfish starter. Tender steak and homemade sorbet. Excellent ambiance, food, and service. Then go for the papers. For the papers. "Georgette lives in Alabama with her best friend and life partner, eight horses, fifteen chickens, one rabbit, five cats, and two dogs. 'I blog, read blogs, and comment on blogs in spurts. Although I am not always consistent, here is a list of bloggers I think are pretty groovy.'" "The Real Sun Myung Moon: Is Barack Obama Running a Cult?" More rubbish: "A Dollar a Day; Presidents and Prison" and "Emotions and Money" and "Who Is Ron Paul/How Can We Salvage The Economy?" and "Hermaphrodites for Clinton" and...

This is why I drink Cat Diesel. You think. This is why I drink Cat Diesel. He says.

He says: "To-day is HST Death Day. I still have that bottle of aged alcohol. We can kill it when you get to Silber-Spraings."

I met Kissinger with Reagan when the Gipper was running for Prez in '80. Shook hands with him in a fruit market just outside Cleveland. Kissinger's hand. The Gip was too busy holding up babies and laying off traffic controllers. That came later, but it's how memories work here. They get mashed up into a 12-quart pot. Carter had just clusterfucked two helicopters on their way to pluck out the hostages from some abandoned kebab joint in Tehran. Operation Eagle Claw. Has landed. Harshly. Both of them. Also of note, the role Canada played in this debacle: Canadian Caper. Kudos to Canadian ambassador Ken Taylor.

Go.

And so we sold fruit to Czechoslovaks and Poles (the curtain hadn't fallen in '80 so they were still called Czechoslovaks) and honed our English language skills while some grade B actor from Tinseltown moseyed around fishing for support.

Cent. Five Cent. Ten Cent. Dollah.

Cent. Five Cent. Ten Cent. Dollah.

CentFiveCentTenCentDollah.

CentFiveCentTenCentDollah.

Only by the time we blurted out "may I help you" (which, incidentally always came out as: MayaaahIhee…), customers had already moved on to the Kelbasa and Flaki wołowe stand. Bloody Poles and their Solidarity. I was eleven when I got hooked to grapefruit. Years later my dentist (a Chinese dwarf with a severe limp) chastised me for eating too much citrus (and ingesting massive amounts of wine). Said it was eroding my teeth. Had little holes in the bones that he drilled without anesthesia and filled with some clear compound/sealer. It was the first time I'd been told too much of a good thing is bad.

He was a tai chi and feng shui master.

And drilled without remorse.

Or numbing gels.

Or gas.

After the fruit stand I snagged a job cleaning out old warehouses downtown. Walked through a curtain of fiberglass every day. It's when I started smoking. Twelve years old. The other boys did it so. So. You know. One of them, Terry, drove a shit Chevy Nova (350 with dual exhaust) and kept girlie mags in the boot. That's the trunk. On lunch breaks he'd go into his car and do his business. Always he came out lighting up a stogie. The shit we cleared out of those warehouses was Eliot Ness junk. Bureaus and armoires and machines from that era. Al Capone times. That kind of rubbish. Ness was a pig, though. A drunkard full of braggadocio who read Sir Arthur Conan Doyle as a kid.

Amazing how Sherlock Holmes drives all of us to the sauce.

You pair tiramisu with a crayfish starter. Tender steak and homemade sorbet. Only my take on it is: chłodnik litewski, barszcz czerwony, rosół z kurczaka, and for a main you go with polędwiczki wołowe. Excellent ambiance, food, and service.

(Bloody Poles and their Solidarność.)

      "MayaaahIhee…"

      "Hey, where's my crabs ye fookin alien?"

      "Grab it, the bucket."

Basil
(Thrush Poetry Journal, July 2012)

He was so old
his bones seemed to float
inside his skin
I went to feel his pulse

he slapped at me and so
instead, I rolled the dice for him
on the backgammon board
and lit his pipe
He sprayed perfume on his palm
and ran it through his hair
How many pigs I slaughtered
in this yard, he said
How many?
While you hid inside the back room
and plugged your ears from the screaming.
How many?
Mis manos
abren las cortinas de tu ser
Octavio Paz
snuck out from around his pipe
through clenched teeth
Under old trees
men lie down again, again

Idiosyncrasy
(Amphibi.us, April 2012)

my father used to cross himself every time we passed a church
it was a strange habit i thought
it didn't matter what the denomination of christianity the church
spewed
he just crossed himself
sometimes at sixty-five miles per hour
it became quite comical
especially if we were travelling through the South
where there's a church it seems every hundred yards or so
i asked him once why he didn't pay his mobile respects
to mosques or hindu temples or synagogues
we had those around our city as well
his answer was defensive convoluted and circular
much as you would expect from an intellectual or academic
(which is what he was)
but to his credit he had read the Qur'an
as well as countless pages of hindu texts
buddhist shinto tao and zen as well
he devoured non christian religious literature as if it were comic
books
my father died at the end of the last century
instead of burying him as he wished
my sisters and i had him cremated
we had very little money and turning someone to ashes it seems
is a better financial choice if you're on a budget
he would have no doubt protested our choice
but
ashes to ashes is how it goes i think
the church to which he belonged all his life
(greek orthodox)
burned to the foundation not long after he died
only the lower third of the giant cross remained
i drove by the site once on my way to settle some accounts
my father had left unresolved

there were two boys rummaging for something just next to the
burned cross
one of them picked up a rock and heaved it at the charred remains
and then they laughed and ran away

In Fifty-Seven Words
(Thunderclap Press, April 2012)

the heat burned my eyes dry
while reading *pomes*
on a commuter train
banking slowly over Philly.
have i made you insane yet
with my bifurcations?
the conductor passes me a note;
a cable like in the old days:
"the fridge froze my salad;
i want some wine."
and man is a bird
made of mud.
stop.

The Men
(Amphibi.us, September 2011)

I read Carver mostly and Bukowski (still)
at those crucial times when I think the walls are breathing me thin
rubbing me out
and the dullness of the gin doesn't help
I used to advertise that
but it contributed to the agony
There were always the usual queries
why do you only read men
why only those two men
aren't you a misogynist like those men you read
And so on into a thick humid night
several nights running
Usually my mistakes ended in some kind of smashing of
something
plates bottles paintings
one time even the old Underwood
(that one really hurt because I didn't have the money to buy
another machine)
So now I don't say anything
I lie
I confess to watching TV
like most of the people I know
But still there are the usual queries
which show
which network
at what time
why do you always watch TV
shouldn't you do something more productive
I have this apocalyptic vision of all the inquisitors
they drive in from work
up their driveways
into their garages
the automatic doors slide down shut
before they even get out of their cars

they go inside their homes through the utility door
and start asking questions
until their loved ones one day pack up and leave
for good.

Magnifying Glass
(Amphibi.us, April 2010)

looking at a woman condemned
in the hospital bed my mother is a fragile carcass of bones and
skin
like leather
i try to see the dignity of having lived her life her own way
smoking herself into the hole
there is still pride in those eyes
fear and pain as well
looking at a woman condemned
i listen to the minutia the details that now construct her present
a tray of food with subpar sustenance
a night nurse who withholds pain medication
a young surgeon who probably drives a Mercedes
obtuse patterns on the carpet
mismatched curtains

when your mother is dying before you
(when anyone is)
there is nothing left to weave for anybody
what you know is lucid and true: you are looking at a condemned
soul
what you do is bide your time
her time
by examining the simple details
through a magnifying glass
and the next day when you come to visit
and you see the wreath the hospital has placed on her door
you know that probably nothing will have changed
outside the building
the trash is still being picked up on Tuesdays
the team of RNs is still out back smoking stogeys
people are getting mugged shat upon cut down by cars
nothing will have changed
outside her room

Miles and Miles

(Thunderclap! Magazine – Issue 7, November 2011)

in my feverish coma i see miles this way. but i don't hear him. monk is out of the frame blowing smoke into my field of vision. so i see miles through monk's cigarettes. and in my ears, competing with the tinnitus, is that old Who song. you know it. the one about seeing for...you know it. i've never heard you blow, i tell miles. not once. he takes his horn and walks upstairs. i hear footsteps on my ceiling. crackling of the wood floor under his wingtips. there is a pause. an auditory pause, as well. as if someone yanked the needle across vinyl tracks. from up above comes a long, muted sound. it's a crane. it could be eric dolphy as a crane. now you've heard me, miles says through the floorboards. i track his footsteps above, going toward the staircase. but he never comes down. miles never comes down.

Sleepers
(Trainwrite, January 2012)

We took a sleeper to Amsterdam from I-don't-know-where because France derailed us with its wines and cognacs and armagnacs. And girls with Gauloises.

I know we paid in Guilders (there was no Euro then) through a small opening at a small window to a shrunken woman with spectacles who then said, "Welcome," but more in the "Welcome to Europe" way than the polite response one usually gives after being thanked.

Halfway through the night, the train stopped I-don't-know-where, Utrecht maybe, Arnhem maybe, Tilburg, Eindhoven, maybe neither, but it picked up an armed band of English hooligans high on their team's win earlier in the day, who stormed into the sleeper and started banging on anything that was made of matter—rattling, shaking, looking to destroy—all the time yelling in fascinating unison: MAN-CHES-TER! MAN-CHES-TER!

They roused everyone to their feet and for one terrifying moment I thought it was 1942 and we were being transported to Dachau. Like cattle.

But as suddenly and violently as the bald heads invaded the car, the wave receded down the line. *Jesus, what was that*, a man with crusty eyes said in solid English. Football. It brings people together.

Writers Inside a Bag / Parabolic Urine Flow
(Airplane Reading, January 2012)

I took Hemingway and Bukowski and Palahniuk and F. Scott and Hitchens with me, and we crossed the border into Canada like the hooligans that we are (F. Scott would object to that, but he's dead so let him howl from beyond). Only, none of them saw the light of day. It must have been savagely boring inside that leather messenger bag for six straight hours of flying. I imagine an omnibus such as that would surely be the cause of one stabbing. Or at least a drunken debacle. Tight quarters, gargantuan egos, and a rattling fuselage. Welcome to the Chelsea Hotel? Indeed. From time to time I dumped a few drops of red wine down to them, to keep them somewhat pacified and well lubricated. Bukowski hates flying. All I was left with, was stained book covers. Please allow me my grey matter short-circuits. I am a bright man otherwise.

The gent next to me at the urinal at YYZ airport started in on an elongated diatribe about the medical profession. He loved it and he loathed it. His mother was an LPN. Or Registered. Things get somewhat fuzzy when one is trying hard to just stand straight and aim into a porcelain cup. To me he confessed: as a child, his urethra was somehow suddenly blocked or fused, and they had to drill his dick. Either the urologists botched the gig, or there were still some ongoing changes to come with the onset of puberty, so he had to be back for the same procedure at age 18.

"Only I refused," he said. "I didn't care about having a crooked stream flow. Do you know what it's like to have a drill down your member?"

I thought about the consequences of curved urine flow, and took a few tiny steps away from him. Turns out his mother still keeps his foreskin in formaldehyde and he now is an expert at reading Tarot cards. He offered a quick reading only I'm not ecstatic about such things right before boarding an airbus. Although the Death Card signals the beginning of a great change, I prefer not to have that drawn in general. I buttoned up and we said our goodbyes. I left him standing, flipping, shaking, and making some sort of circular motion with his hips.

It's quite peculiar what one is privy to in airport washrooms.

Three Decades in an Empty Jar of Mayo
(The Legendary, April 2010)

we were broke then
when lennon got shot
outside the dakota on 72nd then
reagan came along
ushered morning in america
and gave the impression
that we were rich or we could be
hinckley disagreed
and we are broke now then
everything is cyclical
then i watched boxcar willie
sell his greatest hits on the small screen
hart to hart star blazers three's company
love boat fantasy island dynasty tj hooker
fall guy bosom buddies facts of life all trash
listened to queen blondie elvis
(costello not the other one)
clash pistols pretenders talking heads
got my news first from frank reynolds
then peter jennings then roger...roger...moore
no mudd roger mudd
most of them are gone now
holes without holes really
because no one is missed
after enough time flows
no matter how loudly they howl

Half Asleep in Striped Pajamas

(The Legendary, April 2010)

a
hahahaha
the fellas sang at the machine
when i tripped Robbins
Robbins was a shit of a man
in cahoots with Tante Wilfreda
(is what we called her)
found them banging behind a stack of pallets
(Robbins and her)
and got the Little Debbie's man
to take photos
ve maek eet fit
Tante Wilfreda once told me
while i was lifting impossibly heavy boxes
filled with shit from China
materiel
plastic garbage
above my head
on shelves two stories high
in the warehouse
ve maek eet fit
she said
and i fucking hated her
the bloody Nazi exploitative cunt
we got treated like horse shit
all of us
black white foreign domestic poor middle class…
the Coke vendor
looked like Harry Reames
the porno guy from the 70s
who became a preacher in the late 80s
the Coke guy got the Tante fair and square
behind the loading dock outside the warehouse
he came on her chin

and smacked her with his cock
while the weekly Richfood shipment came in
a giant air-conditioned semi
and i swept the aisles
futility
you sick
motherfucker

Welcome Back Bub, We Missed Ya
(The Legendary, April 2010)

moving through the thick air of eight hours
is excruciating
i drive to the job squinting in the 7 am sun
and i think all i want to do is veer off
into the oak tree there
in the median
one more day responsible
for one more task
licking a stamp
or
pulling a lever
filling out a time sheet
little blank squares
these are the things
that take me down
eviscerate me
quickly
howya doin' bub?
how's it hangin'?
long time no see?
glad to see yer mug 'round here
where ya been?
where ya at?
wanna cigarette?
they're turning screws into my flesh
the lot of 'em
and me?
i'm putting out the fires
looking for band-aids
hey Hank
who's gonna save me baby?
this day
seems like two weeks

Sick

(The Legendary, April 2009)

i waited for her at the hospital in the waiting room on the floor on
which she stayed
and watched a team of slow moving cancer patients go round and
round
with their IVs hooked to metal poles on wheels.

they all wore bathrobes which were obtusely opened at the chest
showing scars and knife marks
punctures and bandages
holes and dark flesh bunched up together.

round and round they walked an invisible track
and sometimes they looked like harness racing jockeys
in slow motion.

when she came in she carried a white Styrofoam cup filled with
thin coffee
and complained the night nurse withheld her medication
probably to sell it down the line to some shitty addict waiting in
the garage
in the sub-basement of the building.

want some? it's awful, she said.
it was.
when're you gettin' out i asked
and she shrugged and when she did
her shoulders lifted the eviscerated flesh for a moment under her
robe
for me to see that what it really looked like
was much like the impact point of a grenade that had gone off
under her ribs.

jesus! she said when she caught me looking
and i pulled away embarrassed and flustered.
can't they make a regular goddamn cup of coffee here?

Round Trip to Elyria for a Funeral and Wake

(Lost in Thought Magazine, October 2012)

Linearity.

My time lines are obfuscated now, and people no longer trust me. I have muddied everything into an uneven ball of clay, which I continually try to smooth over, but nothing will work; I have rough palms. People don't believe me. I, myself, can no longer tell the difference between what really happened and what should have happened. Or what didn't happen at all. How I lost change, how I found it, how I cashed it in for banknotes or weird favors. How I swallowed coins when there was nothing else left to eat. I see history as jagged lines, time as circular with weird radii connecting strange, spatial matter outside a sphere. I've let people down. I've brought them up. I've lost them. And in their place I found large, empty, cardboard boxes in which to climb and hide. Only, cardboard gets soft and soggy in a rainstorm. It collapses eventually. And you're left with pulp.

Footprints.

The most divine coaction of the sea is the wave that perpetually comes in and erases the indentation that you've carved with your weight into the wet sand, thinking you've built something. Or you've left something for someone to follow or see or measure. Or judge. You are nothing.

Funerals and Wakes.

Nothing like that is important. Funerals and wakes are for the living. Step back and watch people scurrying and busying themselves like attentive ants, carrying out a plastic tradition of grief and forgiveness. Because it's how it's always been done. Because you don't question at a time like this. Because you're honouring the dead. Even when the dead is dead.

So now I'm washing my hands at the small, pink sink downstairs. I pull the knob to the faucet, which he installed three years ago, just before he died; eviscerated by that ghastly animal that ate him from within his lymph nodes. And I think, that's what we should all leave behind. Faucets that work. That don't drip. Forget children, they'll eventually forsake their parents. Forget your melancholic traditions. They'll eventually consume you properly from the inside out.

Faucets.

He drives. A green, 1981 Chevy Caprice station wagon. We go around and around the freeway, missing our exit and smiling incredulously at the futility of our situation. And we curse some unknown civil engineer with a degree from Purdue University, who has managed to hide the ramp which will take us away from this concrete madhouse, to a small apartment filled with roach eggs stuck to the underside of shelving paper in the cabinets, on the second floor of a garden style walk-up. I sit on the back bench, next to his tools: a plumber's wrench, electrical tape, pliers…and a bow with most of its strings snapped and hanging from one end like a singed horse tail.
"What I miss the most is swimming in the sea."
"Remember that summer we both did the breast stroke among the jellyfish?"
"The boat had a slow leak in the underside…"
"…and we towed it ourselves swimming the two kilometers back to shore."
He says, "One late August a Turkish freighter came by and signaled to pick him up from the water. The sailors offered him a ride and political asylum in Trabzon."
"Why didn't you go?"
"I don't remember," he says. "My time lines are wrong. Now I'm thinking it was in Mexico and the lifeguards were yelling *'peligro,*

peligro' because I was so far out. Sharks, you see."

"And Turkish freighters."

The corrections.

I think I may have told you my father's story; I can't keep
anything straight anymore. I'm a somnambulist; a copy of a copy.
I build and erase constantly. I've lost myself in the fibers of truth
and lies.

"There's our building again," he says.

"The reference point."

And still no sign of the undulated exit. It must be hiding in
someone's pocket.

Upgraded amenities and fixtures.

"Laminar flow increases wetting like an aerated stream but is less
noisy and produces less splash," he says.

"What?"

"I'll show you if we ever find this bloody exit."

I make him promise to bring out the instrument and play a few
bars. Later, when he does, he struggles with the massive wooden
body of the contra-bass. When he concentrates like that a large,
thick vein protrudes from his forehead and pulsates alive with the
blood of music. And I am suddenly watching a man play out his
dreams; a man whose future in this new country has been defined
by water flowing through PVC and CPVC pipes.

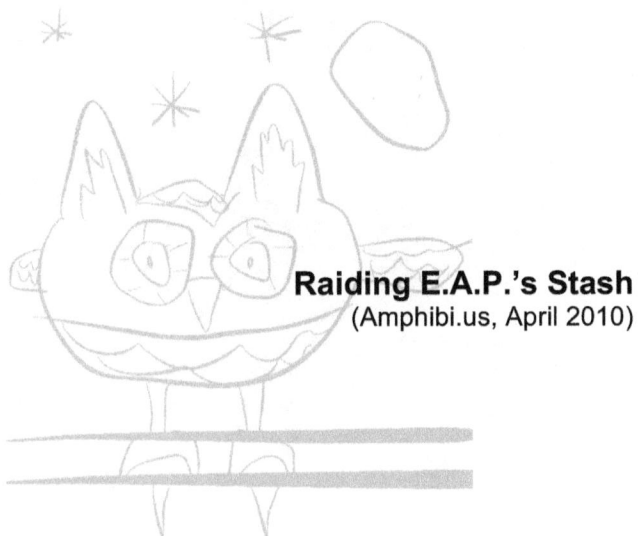

Raiding E.A.P.'s Stash
(Amphibi.us, April 2010)

we staked out Edgar Allan Poe's grave
that late-January night
pints of Mad Dog 20/20 in our breast pockets
and camels hanging from the corner of our lips
marching in place trying to ward off frostbite
we were dying for something good
and Sid had the bright idea of liberating
the fifth of cognac that would be left on Poe's grave that night
in honor of his birthday
some freak in a cape comes every year at midnight
Sid said
and drops off the Hennessey
(i imagined it was william carlos williams resurrected)
free booze you understand?
i did and had no shame about pinching the stuff
after all, Poe wouldn't need it
we stomped in place like Popeye Doyle in that movie scene
to get the blood flowing down to our feet
until we ran out of both juice and smokes
the temps hit in the negatives
and sometime around two in the morning we gave up
or gave in
by the time he drops off the booty we'll be frozen stiff
Sid said
and what in hell good that's going to do?
and so we both shuffled back to our apartment at Loyola
empty-handed
there was a small story in the afternoon edition of The Sun next
day
probably the same one it runs year after year
about a mysterious caped man who leaves a bottle of cognac on
Poe's grave
every January 19th
to this day I'm not sure

whether or not that's one of Poe's most enduring stories
the thing about fiction is
that it's truer than the truth
and so you don't know what to believe
(or maybe you do and you believe it)
what do you think happens to all those bottles
Sid said later in a Pavlovian trance dreaming about the booze
I told him I wasn't sure about the story anymore
you're probably right he said
nobody wears capes nowadays
and anyway
even if it were true
the cops probably confiscate the loot
and give themselves a party with it
probably
I said
Poe's grave is city property
filthy pigs
Sid said
we should go to Key West
it's warmer there
and no one ever goes hungry
they have feral chickens roaming around all day
(and cats with five toes)

Frankie Goes to Hollywood (Redux)

(Jumping Blue Gods, February 2012)

Tinseltown was before I took the IBM job in southern Florida and became a willing corporate casualty of flesh-grinding cogwheels, lobbying for conservative political action committees, and midnight tech meetings around greasy Chinese take-out containers. Pop will eat itself. Tinseltown was before all that. Before I found God cowering in corrugated cardboard boxes and masquerading as postal service carriers or stray dogs or garbage on the side of highways blowing in the hot breeze and letting itself be photographed by some film student with a shitty wind-up camera a la Robert Flaherty who just happened to see some divine Fibonacci sequence in its parabolic dance.

Tinseltown was:

four in the morning, finding fillet and scalloped potatoes in the dumpster, so I'd get to eat at Musso & Frank's, only out back. Back of the house. On fifth and something something, Cenan's Bakery would throw out bagels and baguettes and some other pastry type filo dough shit every Saturday morning so there was that. Carbs. Protein. That's how I ate. I lived with three runaway kids from Ackworth, Iowa and Norman, Oklahoma. Two were American Indian and loved Sherman Alexie. *(offhand: Jesus, did you know Rainer Maria Rilke was black?)*

They ground down pills and shot them into their veins while I drank rubbing alcohol shoplifted from People's drugstore. The Indians called it "Cheyenne Champagne." I let them put cocaine on my lips once and my entire mouth went numb. I tried LSD. A hit and a half and I had a shitty trip looking at myself in the bathroom mirror.

Daing esse, you need a guide when you do that shit for the first tyne.

After that I stuck to rubbing alcohol. Good for the insides. I'm unsure how I can atone for all of it. There was other stuff too, Freon, CO_2...all the while there was an accident waiting for me back home. Back East.

Back East.

Back.

One of the twins didn't make it. He walked about stillborn and got lost in the labyrinth.

Not sure how to reconcile that.

I read things in books like: "Death is the road to awe" and never found comfort in any of it. Some did. The kids in Hollywood did. I dropped my wallet in El Segundo.

Or somewhere around John Wayne airport.

I lived in:

North Hollywood, West Hollywood with the drag queens and dominatrices, prostitutes.

Children.

And then came El Toro and a crazy, armed Serbian immigrant landlord with a Philippine girlfriend who thought I was banging her and who disassembled the lock to my rented room and watched me from a chair just outside my door, through a tiny, drilled hole. Just across, to the west, there was Laguna Beach and a small efficiency flat, and I thought one day I could go to Pepperdine in Malibu and study film or...

literature or...something if I'd only had the money.

How I got out was, I walked to the 405 on Saturday afternoon and got picked up by a car full of girls going to Tempe, Arizona to see the Gin Blossoms. And that was it. That was Hollywood. It might as well have been Krakow or Ingushetia or

Or

Back East.

Which is where I went.

Running West and East with Important Books in Liquor Store Boxes

(The Legendary, February 2011)

Kant and the Platypus. I false-started that one dozens of times. I false-started Kafka, Representative Man. That was in 1991 in Los Angeles. Hollywood. Laguna Beach. El Toro. It's not El Toro anymore, but I tried it all over southern California. It's over six hundred pages; you cannot blame me.

I false-started Camus' The Fall. You can blame me for that. That one clocks in at barely hundred and fifty. But I false-started it.

At a truck stop in Albuquerque, just before going through the most awful, monstrous storm I've ever seen in a rickety Karmann Ghia loaded with boxes and clothes. In Oklahoma City at a Luby's. Eating cold Chinese food for breakfast in Amarillo. Memphis, Nashville, Knoxville, Roanoke.

Always there was some excuse. I can't read Camus while driving standard at eighty miles per hour down the Blue Ridge Parkway. I can't understand Mann while sipping on fatty, nasty, chicken soup in some diner in Tucumcari.

There are literal tumbleweeds rolling through the parking lot. Any time now the Coyote will blow by, chasing the Road Runner. Or some old, leathery Indian will stroll up and offer to sell me a Kachina doll. I don't believe in Hopi and Pueblo cosmology. No thanks.

The big news in Kingman was Arizona State playing Arizona. Lute Olson. That's all I heard. Lute Olson. And I cooked ravioli out of a can in a little copper pan on a portable, electric element; the kind you find on stoves in real apartments. I cooked that rubbish in a Comfort Inn, off Route 40 in the middle of nowhere. Every day for fifteen days.

At the Arizona crater I clipped a rock I wasn't supposed to. Stuck it in my pocket all sly like. Like I was some kind of delinquent astronomer. Geologist. Whatever you call those people who steal rocks from national parks.

Took a piss in the Petrified Forest, too.

At the Grand Canyon the Cocteau Twins muttered

something about Heaven or Las Vegas. Got caught up in a traffic jam snaking up toward Hoover Dam, then down. The septic tank to the caravan in front of me gave out, and all the shit started flowing onto the road. Then we stopped. I couldn't get out of the car for 78 minutes. All around there was a two-inch giant puddle of excrement. The Ghia didn't have air conditioning.

In Barstow:

"I'll give you a blow job for a ride into Westwood."

"It's ok."

"No, seriously."

"It's all right. Just pay for half a gas tank."

In Fort Smith, Arkansas:

"We have the best fried chicken in the entire You-Nited States, sunshine."

"I believe it."

"What's that accent you got?"

Lebanon, Tennessee had girls with the poofiest hair I'd ever seen. They were all nice. But the hair.

Lebanon, Tennessee:

"Whatchu readin'?"

"Nothing. I'm just looking at the same paragraph over and over."

"Yea, but what is it?"

"Depression, I guess."

Petrol ran like this:

Dollar twenty in North Jersey. Ninety-five cents in Kansas City. Ninety cents in Memphis.

Arrowheads ran like this:

Dollar fifty for a small in Estancia, New Mexico. Dollar ninety-nine for a large in Clovis and Gallup.

I traded an old paperback copy of Richard Brautigan's In Watermelon Sugar for a gyro sandwich and a postcard at a gas station in Pulaski. The clerk had been an English major at Virginia Union in Richmond. He gave me a tip and I snagged The Tokyo-

Montana Express later that year from a used bookstore in Westwood. The postcard? I sent that to myself, at the old address in Annandale. In case I changed my mind and went back home. I did, but only nine months later.

"What is it?"

"Nothing."

"Eh, nothing. What?"

"Nothing. Depression, I guess."

Travelin' Light

I once blew through the entire Johnny Mercer songbook racing across the country, east to west, on Rt. 40. Eighty-three hours from D.C. to Los Angeles with a quick hike up to Vegas where I pinched the casinos for $325 and a handful of free seven-and-sevens. Just before, I got caught up in a traffic jam coming down into the desert off Hoover Dam. The caravan directly in front of me suffered a busted septic tank and I slowly drove my Karmann Ghia through dozens of gallons of shit and piss while admiring the prowess of the Colorado River. That was pretty much how things rolled in America for me at the end of the 20th Century: crawling through a river of excrement while enjoying unbelievable geography and time-chiseled red rock.

When Johnny ran out I flipped on the AM. The best way to slice this savage, weird country is in a 60s German car with the amplitude modulation turned on full blast and the windows down. Insane preachers mix in with broadcasts of Mexican soccer matches mix in with conservative fear mongering mix in with insane preachers again. Again. Rinse, repeat, don't rinse.

Los Angeles was a flooded mess when I arrived in February. It was a brutish, carnivorous quadruped with sharp incisors, looking at the rest of us through exotic corrective lenses. It claimed my wallet. In El Segundo I stopped at a gas station to see about a leaky oil pan and the bloody city lifted my billfold right out of my front pocket.

Fuck John Wayne airport. It was there, on the San Diego Freeway, just short of my destination in Irvine, that I got caught up in a traffic jam, which had me waiting four hours to squeak out three miles. I hated Los Angeles. I hated Westwood. I hated Malibu. Pepperdine. El Toro. Laguna Beach. I hated it all. Los Angeles disposed of me in little less than a year. I came rolling back across the country stopping once in Amarillo, Texas where I had the strangest plate of Twice Cooked Pork at a Chinese place in a strip mall off Rt. 40. The meat looked like fried cricket tongues. I cracked open the fortune cookie and left a tip under the teapot.

The little strip of paper read: "You like Chinese food."

Saints

First thing I ever did when I arrived in New Orleans was buy a bottle of cheap bourbon from the ABC to go with the cheap room in the cheap transients' house on Josephine Street just at the edge of the Garden District. I set the bottle on the filthy table by the window and poured the golden juice into a small, dirty tumbler which I had packed in the duffel bag, and listened to Mahler's 5th on my small radio. I watched dozens of streetcars going down St. Charles with happy tourists ready to pop hundreds on drinks and po' boys and shirts and voodoo dolls and...something.

Always something for sale in this goddamn town. Snake oil for the aching joints. Beads to throw in return for a peek at bare tits. People are so goddamn thick. Always, always something. Every bloody town. For sale.

When the booze ran out I crossed the street and sat down at the bar in Igor's and ordered a seven and seven. Hard on the Seagram's and easy on the seven. I put down a tenner. I had money from a tax return that previous year. I had worked. And I had also won three hundred dollars at the roulette in Vegas the previous week. Red fourteen. My only win, aside from the time I hit the trifecta at Pimlico in Laurel my last year in high school. That brought in a bit over two hundred.

Igor's was a great place, right on St. Charles in uptown. It had a big neon sign on the front: "A half pound burger is always waiting for you!" Inside there was the bar and then some: laundry facilities, so you could drink while you washed and dried your loads of stained, infested junk.

The chippie barkeep wore short jean shorts and was all legs. And she knew it. She made sure to exaggerate her squats whenever she'd pick up a bottle from below the counters, and gave a good show to all the barflys smoking the day away. She made a good double-seven, and that's really all that mattered.

There were video poker machines just behind me, and the most decrepit, down-n-outers were pumping coins into the bastards at an alarming rate. Somehow they had money. I drank.

A storm or hurricane or something rolled in.

The barkeep shift changed and the chippie disappeared into the laundry facilities. Some woman next to me snorted and said she was probably turning tricks upstairs, the whore. That's what she called her.

There was a room above the bar you could rent by the hour or day, she said. I just drank. The rain came hard outside and we couldn't hear the jukebox with the door open like that. It sounded like some giant waterfall in Argentina.

"About time," the new barkeep said.

He was an old dog with boils on his nose and cheeks and when he poured, his hand shook and spilled booze all around the shot glass. He cleaned it up with a yellowing rag. He also blew his nose with it. Right in front of everyone.

"About time," he said again first looking at me and then quickly swinging his head toward the window. Gusts were spraying water into the bar but no one got up to close the door.

"Yeh heh?"

"I like it. Rain comes in and washes all the scum away. All the shit and piss on these cursed streets. The saints and ghosts and pimps..."

I tuned him out and cross faded him with Travis Bickle: "All the animals come out at night—whores, skunk pussies, buggers, queens, fairies, dopers, junkies, sick, venal. Someday a real rain will come and wash all this scum off the streets."

Nothing changes. Not even the weather. I left after half an hour of being bothered by a soliloquizing former pirate who had lost everything in a divorce and was looking for work as a carpenter, only he wasn't really looking. None of us are. All he did was talk and smoke my cigarettes. And so I left.

Later I walked by Fritzel's in the French Quarter and heard Terrence Blanchard inside. I couldn't afford the ticket. But he was brilliant for those fifteen seconds I hung around before the big goons came out to sweep the sidewalk clean of transients. And so it goes.

Chicory coffee and two beignets at Café Du Monde for buck-ninety and some lonely soul at midnight telling me how beignets ought to be made with cottonseed oil and how chicory was developed by the French during their civil war because coffee was scarce during those times, and they found that chicory added body and flavor to the brew.

"The Acadians from Nova Scotia brought this taste and many other French customs to Louisiana..."

I cross-faded him with...I couldn't. He was adamant.

"Chicory is the root of the endive plant..."

I couldn't make him stop. He wanted fifty cents for his history lesson.

"Don't have fifty cents."

"How 'bout a dollar?"

And that got him to walk away and start in all over again at a table of well-fed, nocturnal warrior-tourists. Always something for sale in every bloody town. Always. Cute little black kids tap dancing on the corner: 75 cents. Man blowing into a rusty sax needs a new reed: dollar. Man with box of shoe polish and brushes: "Skew me. Skew me, sir, you dropped somethin'."

"What?"

"You dropped your shine! Deluxe job on the go with wax and moisture protection: Five twenty-five. Shit, son...people got to make a living."

I took the streetcar back up St. Charles and jumped off at Josephine. There was a group of frat boys pissing on the side of a building, laughing and screaming something about going backdoor on some girl one of them had met, and how much she'd like it from all of them. Nothing ever changes. People are mostly shit to one another. Even the cockroaches exploit the other cockroaches. I went to my room, sat at the table in the dark and turned on the radio. They were playing The Blue Danube waltz; von Karajan conducting.

Veracruz in Fragments
(The Rusty Nail, July 2012)

We met him downstairs in the hotel bar. He was working on a Martini with a spiral onion floating in it. A Gibson, maybe, is what they call it. Wolfgang thought he might be worth something. "I'm Seu," he said. "I'm from Sao Paolo. You know where that is from, man?"

"Yea."

"I facking hate this Mexico. Brasil is number one." He held up his index finger and jabbed the air above. "You like futbol?"

"Yea."

"Is number one. But in Sao Paolo, you haves to walk with bodyguards, man. You know why?"

I told him I had friends in Rio and knew all about the kidnappings and the ransoms. He asked if they needed good bodyguards. I told him they probably didn't. They probably had the best security in town. My friends' parents owned a mining company.

"What mine?" he said. "For what? The fossils? The gas?"

"Mica."

"Ah, of course," he said and put his hand on Wolfgang's knee.

Later we went to his suite and inhaled Freon. He killed a few lines of blow and then he put on a porno tape. After a while, Wolfgang got up and followed him into the bedroom. I popped the tape out and watched Alf, dubbed in Spanish. I sat on the couch and smoked Indonesian clove cigarettes and drank Irish whisky and waited for them to finish their business.

"They found that Brazilian guy in the alley back behind the Chicken Man's shack," Wolfgang said.

"Really?"

"Yea. All jacked up. They cut off his balls and stuck them in his ears."

"Jesus."

"Goddamn savages," Wolfgang said.

"What you think he got into?"

"Shit, who cares? These fuckers always got something nasty going on. He should've gone out with a bodyguard," Wolfie said and laughed.

"Let's get a drink downstairs."

"You shoulda clipped that can of Freon, you useless cunt. I could use a good battery high."

In the afternoon we went to the pool and smoked cloves. I hung a towel over my head to save my brain from the sun.

"We ought to go to the beach, for Chrissakes," he said. "Been here three days and haven't set foot on the beach."

"All right."

"It's black, you know."

"What?"

"The beach. It's black."

"Oh yea?"

"Yea. It's volcanic sand."

"Really? I've never seen that."

"You provincial gypsy fuck. All you people ever talk about is the Black Sea and corn on the cob. You ever actually go anywhere?"

I spat just next to him to show off the practical, savvy side of the mother country.

"Classy. But seriously. We ought to go," Wolfie said and crushed the butt of his cigarette on the concrete.

"All right. We should get a drink first."

We sat on chaise lounges on the black beach sipping five-cent Coronitas and read about some American fat cat getting picked off by a Russian-made pistol fired straight into his temple in the early Mexican morning outside Boca del Rio. I adjusted my headdress and Wolfgang said: "Christ, you look like Lawrence of Arabia."

"Seven Pillars of Wisdom."

"What?"

"Nothing. It's the book he wrote."

"The book who wrote?"

"T.E. Lawrence."

"Who?"

"Lawrence of Arabia."

"I'm talking about the movie," Wolfgang said.

"I know."

"What in hell does that have to do with a book?"

"Nothing. Let's get another drink."

The barkeep was a pretty, brown Mexican woman with no front teeth. Wolfgang had to look away each time she smiled.

"It's like the goddamn Wild West," Wolfgang said later, out of nothing. "And stay away from the green cabs. I'm fuckin' telling you. You've been warned."

"El Tajin later? You know, to complete the tour. Like proper Gringos."

"The hell is that?"

"The pyramid."

"They have pyramids here?"

"Yea. They're different. They're Aztec. They got steps."

"I don't know."

"They have temples and altars, too."

"Blood shed, little girl sacrifices, and all that shit?" Wolfgang said.

"Probably."

"All right, let's go."

At Zempoala he had his first breakdown, feeling stifled by the gang of *federales* with machine guns milling about the site. I had to grab him by the shoulders to stabilize the tremors, and we took a cab back to the hotel. Halfway there it started pouring heavy rain and I thought the wall of water was going to crack the windshield. I held him to keep from shaking the whole way over. The cab driver kept looking back at us in the rearview and I thought we were likely going to be eviscerated by his fish-gutting knife for the shitty change we had in our pockets.

In the small Polaroid, Wolfgang is shaking my hand across the net, mocking the professionals at Roland Garros. The paint lines on the court are peeling and there are tall weeds growing from the cracks in the green asphalt at the baselines.

"We've got to get out of this god awful fucking country," Wolfie said.

"Why? What's wrong?"

He slapped a roll of dollars on the table.

"I can't take this shit. I can't fuck these guys anymore."

"Why? What happened? Did you get in a jam with that old rich fag?"

"Nah, that went fine," Wolfie said and lit up a joint.

"What then?"

"We just…we need to get out of here. This place…I don't know. We just gotta go. We gotta go now. We gotta go home. We don't belong here. They don't want us here."

"Listen, it'll be all right. We don't belong home, either. You're just going through some shit, that's all."

"This guy…he had silver teeth," Wolfie said and started to pace. "…like the Devil."

"What guy?"

"The old guy. The rich one. Like the fucking Devil."

"Come on with the Devil. It'll be all right."

"Silver teeth. Silver teeth is fucked up. My grandfather had silver teeth."

"It's all right. Wolf. It'll be ok."

"Fuckin' teeth."

"We'll go to the bar and have a drink."

"We got to go home. Fuck the bar. I can't do this anymore. I want to go home."

I drove back to Mexico City while Wolfie slept in the back seat. We had to share the narrow road with a battalion of horse drawn buggies and carriages. It took us almost eight hours. Wolfie woke up once, as we passed the VW Bug factory in Puebla. He wiped his nose and switched sides on the bench. I looked in the rearview and thought he was sobbing. If he was, he was doing it quietly. I didn't know what to say. The mud huts on the side of the road and the horses and peasants reminded me of my country.

We flew back to Philly. Wolfie's money bumped us up to first class. He slept the entire flight. We sat across from a famous rock singer. He was a grotesque looking man with horrible big lips and long, curly, frizzy hair. I wasn't happy to be back in the States. Twice I had to keep the roll of cash from sliding out of Wolfie's pocket. He just slept.

Last I had heard, he was delivering pizzas in Tempe, Arizona. He was living with a fifty-nine-year-old bisexual man who would drink and rape him repeatedly. I don't know why he stayed there.

In the Polaroid, Wolfgang is shaking my hand across the net, mocking the professionals. He is happy. On the back of the picture, in small, near perfect calligraphy he has written: "How's it all going to end?" And then, underneath that: "Veracruz, 1986."

Señora De Las Iguanas
(Yareah Magazine, April 2012)

It's a straight line across the Isthmus of Tehuantepec, north to southeast.

(I still love Mexico.)

You go from Veracruz right down to Juchitan de Zacagoza.

You go in a yellow 1968 Volkswagen Beetle with a broken cassette player and a furry rabbit's foot dangling from the rearview.

You go past adobe and mud huts and smoke an Indonesian black clove.

And another.

And another.

There is no illusion of time, just the Mexican countryside rolling at one hundred kilometers an hour.

You think: this is what it's like in my own country, so you're not shocked when you see outhouses, poverty, clotheslines.

I love Mexico.

Misery is somehow transcended here.

By what? By whom?

God?

In Juchitan you hit the Pacific Ocean where you catch the sun going into the water.

Coronita beer is five cents at the Salvador bar where a beautiful, brown, Mexican woman with a missing front tooth smiles and serves you even though you're sixteen years old.

Juchitan is in Oaxaca province.

It's an ancient, communal, matriarchal society.

It's fiercely independent.

Everything that is run by women is beautiful.

Everything that is done by women is beautiful.

The goat's dance precedes the slaughter, and even that is sadly prepossessing and resplendent.

You watch the blade slowly go into the flesh and don't turn away.

Grandfather did it that way, too.

Only he needed help to hold down the swine.

And the animal's cries were horrendous.

Do you remember that?

I told you about that; about how when I was a child, I'd run to the room at the back of the house and cover my ears and hum.

But the women even slaughter beautifully.

They give life so elegantly.

And take it back just the same.

You are in Juchitan to try to see through Graciela Iturbide's eyes.

Only you cannot.

You can just recall her photographs.

And listen to the women of the town spin their tales: *Long ago there were two hunchbacks. One was kind but the other was mean and spiteful. The two hunchbacks could not work in the village because everybody made fun of them; therefore they went into the hills to cut wood. That is, the kind one cut all the wood since the mean and spiteful one was very lazy and was always telling his companion:*

—Ay!, how sick I am today. It is better if you go and cut the wood this week. His partner, being kind-hearted, would go into the mountains and do all the work week after week...

That was Domingo Siete.

Well, part of it.

The woman who sat with me and told me that tale also used a needle to dig out a splinter from under my skin.

On my finger.

She sterilized it in the fire in her home.

She told other stories while she worked the needle into the flesh and somehow never drew blood.

El Principe Oso, Blanca Flor, El Conejito Verde.

And El Chupacabra.

Not the tale, but the drink.

Banana, orange juice, pineapple juice, guava juice, and rum.

Clemencia y José:

—Very long ago there lived a couple that had a daughter named Clemencia. The mother, who was a witch, did not like Clemencia because she said the girl was a fool who was always going to church...

A fool. Always going to church.

She tells you about Graciela Iturbide.

–She went back to your country to photograph Texas.

You say.

–That is not my country. I don't have a country.

And then she laughs because she knows you're just a child.

Speaking in child tongues.

Speaking child words.

She says.

–*Mi hijo*, everybody belongs somewhere. Even if in the end, it's just in the earth.

Super-Exchanger

(Slingshot Litareview, January 2011)

The Idea Man.

This is what they call me in their plush offices. But they're
wrong. They don't know anything about sociology or
anthropology, rumours, sneakers, the power of translation,
connection, context. I tolerate them and I don't tolerate them;
either way, they're wrong. They pay me. They love my dreads.
They love that I'm a white guy with dreads. (They think it's cool.
Hip. Edgy. Young. They're wrong.) They love my:
Chucks/Airwalks/Diesels/Hush Puppies/whatever it is I tell
them is cool. Or whatever it is I tell them the kids think is cool. I
say that: The Kids. The kids are all right. I fit an idea. Their idea.
I'm an outside product. Mostly they love that when I'm done with
it, their product gets sold by container-loads. I create the tipping
point for their epidemic. This is what I tell them in their meetings
in their fancy conference rooms with their fancy croissants and
bagels and lox rotting in those awful kitschy woven baskets.
    "Hey, there he is: The Idea Man!"
    I say things like "holmes" or "ciao" or both: "ciao, holmes."
I shower every other day. I use Tom's Apricot under my arms.
Eat hot pockets drenched in Thai chili sauce in their break rooms.
If you crank that shit in the microwave you leave behind the
smell. The olfactory system is the most powerful tool for
recollection and nostalgia. And the most influential. Pretty soon
they're all going down to the Pick-n-Pay and grabbing frozen Hot
Pockets. Lean Pockets. Pot Pie Pockets. Pizza Minis. And so I sell
them microwaveable turnovers from Nestle on the side. Double
up on the paychecks. Hey. Do you blame me? I'm The Idea Man.
Only I'm not. They're wrong. They're the Idea Man.
    I'm just a super-exchanger.
    Just.
    Without me, Idea Men aren't shit. Idea Men are conceptual,
ethereal buffoons. They're nothing. They're on TV, is what they
are. Flexing their fictitious muscles for Sterling-Cooper or some

other shitty made up glamorized bullshit ad agency. Keep watching TV. Keep dreaming of a white Christmas. Idea Men aren't shit without the super-exchangers. Without me.

In 1996 I was living on the streets of Baltimore. Squatted in this abandoned sewing factory on The Block, a crappy area known for prostitution and heroin addicts. The city started a program where they sent a bus every week with clean syringes to distribute to the dope fiends, hoping it would cut down the spread of HIV. It was an exchange program. Deal was you got a clean needle for every dirty one you turned in. But the problem they didn't foresee was they were dealing with addicts. And addicts aren't the most reliable, organized, punctual animals in the kingdom. The other thing was, addicts go through a needle a day; shooting up five or six or seven times. Enough that they dull down the tip so badly, the needle becomes useless. That's a lot of needles. How can a bus coming around once a week possibly serve the needs of most addicts?

Idea Men aren't shit.

Enter the super-exchangers.

Watch: so the city sent out some smart guys from Johns Hopkins—some epidemiologists—along on the bus rides to try to figure out why the program wasn't working. And what those Einsteins observed was a handful of guys coming by each week and dropping off backpacks upon backpacks full of dirty needles at a pop. Five, six hundred syringes in one trip. Far more than they could've used themselves, obviously. And these guys, then, would go back to the street and sell the clean needles for a buck a pop. The bus became a kind of syringe wholesaler. The real retailers were these handful of guys—these super-exchangers— who were patrolling the streets and shooting galleries, picking up dirty needles and making a half-ass living selling clean syringes to addicts.

At first, some of the program's coordinators freaked out: how can taxpayers' money subsidize the habits of heroin addicts?

But then they realized that they had inadvertently stumbled upon a natural solution to the problem they had. And they let the program roll. It was a much better system with super-exchangers handling the distribution this way. How? A lot of people shoot on Friday and Saturday night and they aren't going to necessarily plan to have clean tools ahead of time. The bus doesn't come by when they need to shoot; the bus comes by once a week. And certainly it doesn't stop around shooting galleries. But the super-exchangers can be there at times when junkies are doing drugs and when they need clean needles.

The super-exchangers provide service twenty-four seven.

These Hopkins guys figured out that super-exchangers represented a very special and distinct group. They were unusually socially connected. They knew the streets of Baltimore, they knew the shooting galleries.

They knew the kids who needed clean needles. They knew when.

They were the connectors.

Without them, the Idea Men were shit. The Idea Men were light, tenuous fairies sitting comfortably in their executive chairs with their feet up on the mahogany scratching their hairy balls, drinking martinis, and banging the girlie interns. The Idea Men were the clinical, academic Sterling-Cooper.

And everyone wants to be Sterling-Cooper, that's the problem. You get a shitload of competition.

Me?

I don't know...I like Thai chili sauce on my hot pockets.

I bet you do too.

I bet.

Urban Legend
(Girls With Insurance, May 2010)

(pt.1)

If you're looking for something nice-nicey to digest, then you can just stop right here. I can't do it for you. I can't give you the "summer read." I can't get my shit together to print out documents. I can't even burn them anymore. And so, if you want something good and nice...go to the Chick Lit section. Rif lit. Light lit. Beach reading. Whatever they call it now.

I have four stacks of single-spaced paper with verbal diarrhea on them. Words, like. Probably over a hundred and eighty thousand. At last count. The way to go about it normally would be to start sifting through all of it and picking and eviscerating. But I can't. I can't even leaf through the damned thing. This is my sofa. You know those guys, those pack rat bachelors who drag along their shit sofa with holes and broken frames and springs? Those sofas that smell like foul ass? That's me and my stack of written papers. Stories. Last year I burned some of them in a pit outside, but I can't even get motivated to do that. I can't even start a fire, much less throw pounds of paper into it. This is my ass-smelling sofa.

On weekends I sign sponsor sheets. Twelve-steppers. Alcoholics, sex addicts, pedophiles, druggies. Whatever. They give me their official sheets and I throw down my John Hancock. And off they go to their support groups. It's my repentance. Sponsorship of the downtrodden. It's how I set things straight with God. I had to re-read that. It makes me laugh. Doesn't it?

What I send out now is made up shit in the form of urban legends. If you've heard any of them, you've read my work. The cell phone one where people pop raw corn is my latest. A phone company bought that one and made a video out of it. I got a residual in the mail for my work. Only the way I originally wrote it, it was an egg that got cooked. Egg in the middle of two cell phones ringing. Or better yet, four mobiles. Someone dials the individual numbers, phones begin to ring. Egg gets cooked. That's it. It was viral. That's what they call it: viral. The 809 area code scam, that was mine too. The Ashley Flores one. Aspartame as the substance responsible for an epidemic of diseases. Coca-Cola becomes carbonated by accident. Coca-Cola as an effective spermicide. Drug runner evades detection by driving a black, fast truck at night while wearing night vision goggles. The gang known as The Crips take their name from an acronym for "Continuous Revolution In Progress." Its gang members depositing a lethal mixture of LSD and strychnine on pay phone buttons. All of them are mine. Of course, now they're debunked fast by various sources, but still. It's an addiction. It's a vindictive addiction. Middle finger to society. Some people send computer viruses. I send them in stories. We're all addicts. Some of us manufacture the drugs, and some use them. And some do both. Those are the real degenerates. Let the roaches cannibalize themselves. Are they? It beats sifting through two hundred thousand words, trying to pick the best of the best to send out to some gentrified brownstone in Harlem where a privileged twenty-year-old decides which and what to publish in his hip rag. The one about the man who uses his sperm to seal envelopes sent to various government offices. A human penis is found in a jar of fruit punch. Restaurant after-dinner mints contain urine from customers who fail to wash their hands. A girl requires surgery after swallowing a wire that had come loose from a barbecue grill cleaning brush, and was cooked into a hamburger. Baby carrots are made from deformed full size carrots that have been permeated with chlorine. All of them are mine. All debunked, but still…we're all addicts of some sort. I write them to get off, you read them. Food contamination works best. I've done my most brilliant work sending out rumours like this. Insects and weird bugs work well, too. Girl in India wakes up with an inflammation or trauma to her eye. Turns out a spider laid eggs just under her eyelid while she was sleeping and now she has baby spiders filing out of her left retina. And then there's that one about the guy who sits in his apartment at the computer, naked, making up shit and sending it across into cyberspace. He's an addict too. Like all the others. Like all the ones who read his stuff.

(pt. 2)

You can believe that one if you want. The one about the guy with the 70s permed bush sitting naked at his computer and sending off Urban Legend viruses via spam. You can even believe he owns a Velvet Elvis print. It's hung just above the monitor. It's from Turkey, so it's called El Vishnu. Or from Mexico—El Vez. Believe. Or not. I sign them all the same anyway. I always wanted to have X for a middle initial. It's a pseudonym. It's not even unique. I stole the name from that guy who writes for the New Yorker. I mixed up the last name a bit, though.

Sometimes I get cutesy and sign off: "France's Ex." But mostly it's the regular way. With the X in the middle.

Japanese software replaces Microsoft error messages with haiku poetry. Joining Wordofmouth.org will enable you to find out what others are saying about you. Apple is marketing the iLoo, an Internet capable portable toilet.

OK that last one sucked. But I sent it out anyway. "France's Ex." It's like a tag at the bottom of graffiti. I fancy myself that, a graffiti artist. No I don't. I wouldn't say I'm a failed writer though. I haven't failed. I still write. Just in a different genre. You know those guys who make loads of money from their essays, and tour on Spoken Word circuits? You know them. Eric Bogosian, Henry Rollins, Jello Biafra, Laurie Anderson, Hedwig Gorski and all those others? Yea, I wouldn't say I'm a failed writer. Just on a

Spoken Word circuit. A Written Word. Not really a failure, really.

Temple Baptist Church was built on land sold for fifty-seven cents; the amount saved by a little girl who had been turned away from its Sunday school for having a mother who was prostituting herself. Having survived a horrific storm, a slave trader promptly gave up his livelihood, became a Christian, and penned the hymn "Amazing Grace."

It's glurge. It's a sub-genre. Think of it as chicken soup with several cups of sugar mixed in. It's supposed to be a method for delivering a remedy for what ails you by adding sweetening to make the cure more appealing, but the result is more often a sickening sweet mixture that plunges you into hyperglycemic fits. In ordinary language, glurge is the dissemination of inspirational and supposedly true tales; ones that often conceal much darker meanings than the uplifting moral lessons they purport to offer, or undermine their messages by fabricating and distorting historical fact in the guise of offering a true story:

Child badly injured in an accident is comforted by "birdies," his description of angels. William Waldorf Astor rewarded a hotel manager's kindness by making him the manager of the grand Waldorf-Astoria. A war-separated couple is reunited by a tablecloth—an heirloom looted by the Nazis. Description of how laundry was done in bygone days imparts "count your blessings" message.

Glurge. People slop. The more religious intonations, the better. It helps to know history a bit to write this. It also helps to have insomnia and trawl around the cracked streets at night, looking for Jolly Ranchers—Apple flavor.

So one night around midnight I'm driving around somewhere

down near Gaffney. As I come through one of your average little southern towns, I realize that I have a pair of near-crisis situations I need to resolve. I'm almost out of cigarettes, and I have completely run out of hard candy. Have you ever noticed that if you buy a Jolly Rancher bag with all of the different flavors in it there will be like…470 watermelon-flavored and maybe three apples? Yea. I hate that. You can buy a bag with nothing but apple-flavored ones in it, but they only sell them that way in one store I know of down here. Food Lion.

Fortunately, you pretty much can't swing a dead cat in South Carolina without at least spattering a Food Lion establishment with some kitty innards. The little town I'm in has a Food Lion right there on the main street, so I pull in.

So there I am, in the candy aisle, just across from the school supply shelves, checking out the assortment. The store is nearly empty so there's only one other guy in the aisle with me, and he's down there by the school supply end staring at something. Pretty normal looking guy, really. He has on dark gray pants and a crisp looking white button-up shirt. No tie.

Whatever. After 30 seconds or a minute of checking out candies I hear this heavy sniffing sound. It's not really loud, but it's good enough to hear it. So out of the corner of my eye I look down there, and Mr. Normal has a box of crayons in his hand. Your average Crayola-brand 16-pack of crayons. More to the point, he's holding this box of Crayons up to his face, and he's smelling it. I mean really, really smelling it. Like, he starts with his nose at the bottom of the box and then works his way all the way up to that tab at the top, inhaling the whole way. Mr. Normal is standing down there with a box of crayons, and he's sniffing the hell out of these things.

But, saying he's sniffing them doesn't really do it justice, because Mr. Normal is really enjoying this sniffing, you know? If he'd had his shoes off, you probably could have seen his toes curling every time he hoovered that box. A hard-on for sniffing. An addict. And a big, long exhalation thing. You ever smoked a real Cuban cigar? You know how you exhale after you've got it lit and you get that first really good, satisfying drag? Yea.

On the one hand I have a deep desire to get the hell out of there and give Mr. Normal some privacy with the objects of his devotion, but I'm too fascinated to move, you know? I can just imagine accidentally making a noise or something and having Mr. Normal turn around and scream "You're RUINING it for me you fuckin' yuppie!!" and clipping me with his .38. So, basically, I do the only thing I can think of. I freeze and I let this man go to work.

I think I'm there just like that for at least a few minutes, watching this guy savor these crayons. Eventually, he puts the box down gently, almost reverently, and he grabs another one. Slowly, cautiously, almost lovingly, he opens the top of the second pack, eases a few crayons out into his hand, holds them up to his face, and he starts licking them. I don't mean tasting here. I don't mean just like you might put your tongue on something to see if you could eat it. I mean, I'm standing there in the school supplies/candy aisle at Food Lion in middle-of-buttfuck South Carolina and this momo is licking the crayons. Caressing them. Whispering to them. Gently and sensually.

So after Mr. Normal finishes licking the snot out of each and every single crayon in his hand, he gently restores them to the box, closes the box, and puts them back on the shelf. For some child, some toddler, some innocent little kid to pick up later. So I go to have a little talk with the manager.

But the guy is helming down a fucking Food Lion on the night shift. All he cares about is having enough Diet Cokes on the shelves. Spicy Doritos right next to them. I begin to tell him what's going on, but only get as far as the location of the incident, when he puts out his hand. He pulls up his pants by the belt, over his hips, and says:

"Is that sum-a-bitch over there licking them goddamn crayons again? 'Cause if he is, I'm a call his goddamn P.O. and have him go back to jail. I done told him a hunnerd times to stop coming in here doin' that noncent. They's kids that buy them damned things."

I ask what he's out on parole for and the manager licks his lips and leans in and says quietly:

"Fool's a workin' at the Taco Bell two year ago? He done put some roach eggs in the goddamn meat 'cause he ain't like the manager, and made some girly's mouth go all infected with it. Salivary glands, they say at the hospital. All infected. You belie-dat?"
–Francis X. Kline

(pt. 3)

"Dude, you've got patches of hair growing on your back. Like Bigfoot or something. Eddie the Yeti from the Serengeti. The sasquatch with a watch."
That's Benny.
"Huh?"
"On your back. Patches. Like fur stuck on glue or something...like...what the hell?"
"Oh yea? Maybe you shouldn't watch me get dressed. There's something not right about that anyway."

"But the strange thing is…" and he leans in closer, "…they're only popping up on the left side. Huh. That's gnarly. You must have some sort of hormonal disorder thing."

"Fuck you."

By the time you finish reading this sentence, Benny'll ask for a cigarette.

"Dude, can I bum?"

I give him one.

"Fucking menthol? Dude. Please."

That's Benny.

"Got any fire?"

I hand him the lighter.

"Keep it."

He says: "So what time's this thing happening?"

This thing happening is me and Benny going to see my father. Only he is me and I'm the nephew sliding into college on partial scholarship. Partial. But then there's books and a food card and monthly parking money. That's how we play it this time. Before, Benny was the accountant and I was the orderly. I had to change him, my father. He'd pissed all over himself. I had to change him. I was the orderly. And the month before that, Benny was the director of Sunny Vale Assisted Living and I was the liability attorney. Sunny Vale. That's like that box of raisins, isn't it?

"When's this thing happening? Dude. Are you paying attention?" I pull a fancy polo shirt over my T-shirt. To look collegiate and all. Benny takes a long drag and blue smoke comes out his nose. "Dude?"

The thing with my father is, he just doesn't remember. That's how we fleece him. Today Benny is me and I'm the nephew. I'm never me. I can't. He'd never give me anything if I told him I was me. If you think I feel shitty about this, maybe you ought to go back to watching TV. Sign into Facebook and poke somebody. Send them a virtual bouquet of flowers. Pluck your eyebrows. I stopped feeling bad about this right around the time my old man put his fist into my eye socket and rearranged my cheekbone. When I was twelve.

"How much you think this time Dude?"

"Stop flicking ashes on the floor. Use that can."

"Dude, I'm still drinking out of that."

"Fucking...Benny!"

"You want me to put ashes into my beer?"

"Benny!"

Benny's set. He only comes along because he loves me. All right, that's bullshit. Let him tell you:

"Dude, all I ever wanted to do was to be an actor. Hoffman. DeNiro. Fucking Olivier. Dude, OLIVIER: STELLA! STELLA!"

"That's not Olivier."

"Aww, Dude...how can you say that..."

There you go. Benny may be a first class moron but he's set. His father invented the Cube Lube back in 1982.

"Fucking eh!"

Fucking eh. No joke. It was some sort of lubricant specially formulated for the Rubik's Cube. It worked on that pyramid thing too. He incorporated himself into a one man S-corp and called it Bougé Industries, Inc. The way Benny tells it, he meant Bourgeoisie but he was too dense to look it up. It still sounded French with that acute accent and all, so he went with it. He ran his outfit from his garage in New Paltz, New York. Got a P.O. Box where the checks came. Anyway, he made a killing with the Cube Lube. Seems like they all do, don't they? Clueless Gumps falling backwards into bags of cash. Why couldn't I think of something like that. Fucking Cube Lube. Instead, I gotta go scheme out my delusional old man at some country club nursing home.

"Assisted living, Dude."

"Are you listening in on me Benny?"

"Haha."

And he lights a joint.

He says, "You look mah-velous, you preppy frat fuck."

I say, "What'd you do with the cigarette butt?"

He says he dropped it into the beer can, only he's holding it and drinking out of it. And he gives me a smug, stupid smile.

Momos, all of them.

Gumps with boxes of chocolates walking around in bliss.

I say: "Let's go."

Benny needs motivation, scene, and time to get into character.

"Who am I supposed to be again, Dude?"

(pt. 4)

66.6

This is the mile marker on the odometer at which I find God. Where I find God is, on a large, highway billboard, off 40 West; the gigantic sign piercing the parking lot of the Our Perpetual Lady of Sorrow Something Something Baptist Church in Mebane. "Looking for a second chance?" the thing says in two-story, white letters. And then a cyclopean arrow pointing down toward the ground.

Hell.

My guess is the blockheads wanted this clever piece of marketing to include the arrow pointing at the church building, but instead got the hard and fast version from Herb Tarlek.

Hell?

But my guess comes at nearly 90 miles per hour, so there's not much time for reflection, refraction, cogitation, or any of that other bullshit literary mother sauces the French were so good at.

See also: Jean Paul Sartre.

See also: Andre Gide.

Mile marker 66.6.

Right about now I could use a second chance. Third. Fourth. In God's waiting room He's playing Barry Manilow's "Copacabana." Chuck Mangione's "Hill Where the Lord Hides."

Air Supply's "Even the Nights Are Better."

The billboard inviting all the lost souls to join Pastor Xavier Rafer Wilmington Jr. every Wednesday night and twice on Sundays, is quickly succeeded by some horrid, orange Hooters sign saying something about family friendly and chicken wings.

Mile marker 66.7.

"Who am I supposed to be again, Dude?"

That's Benny from the last one. Benny Blanco. His stage name. His driver's license says Bernard K. White. Male. Twenty-seven years of age. Wears corrective lenses. "Other" for race. And so, my Benny. Benny Blanco. Not much of a stretch.

"Like John Leguizamo's character in…"

Carlito's Way.

I know. I went to film school. We took down and eviscerated Dziga and Leni and Maya and both the goddamn Lumiére brothers—Auguste and Louis and their fucking train arriving into the station. So *Carlito's Way* is not a big stretch. During *Battleship Potempkin*, some squash head, black turtleneck and Doc Martens freak kept talking about Einstein. Einstein broke the X-axis rule. Einstein employed a circular cinematic visual trick.

Only it's Eisenstein.

Fucking black turtlenecks and Doc Martens. In film schools.

"Dude, are you paying attention?"

I tell him he's supposed to be me.

In a splenetic, anarchic glee Benny says, "Dude, that's like…feeding John Barrymore that 'nobody puts Baby in the corner' line. That's how wicked that is. You know that line?"

And I do. I went to film school. Nobody got to put Baby in the corner. Not even Jerry Orbach.

Photographs depict damage to automobiles caused by exploding aerosol cans. Photographs show a man falling from a skyscraper while occupants grasp at him through a window. Video shows car striking another vehicle at an intersection, sending the second car into a pedestrian. Security camera footage shows a man with briefcase crossing railroad tracks, absentmindedly talking on a cellphone, suddenly being struck by a commuter train at station in Montauk.
I call these Fauxtography.

(Whaddya call a walking Armenian? A pedestrian.)

Photographs show a KKK member being treated by an all-black emergency room staff. Video clip shows Marc Ecko tagging Air Force One. Photograph shows an enormous, mutant cat raised by a Canadian hermaphrodite. A 119-pound coyote is killed in New York. Photograph shows a parachutist about to drop into a pond surrounded by alligators.

How I feel is…
"Dude, are you listening?"

(pt. 5)

I am listening. I can follow two conversations at the same time. Benny's nonsense as well as my own.
Everything is a potential story.
1983: Burger King opens on Governor's Island and serves beer.
No Fear, Inc., a popular retailer, is being confused with the National Organization for European American Rights (N.O.F.E.A.R.), a white supremacist group.
The state of Missouri names a stretch of highway adopted by the

Ku Klux Klan, the "Rosa Parks Highway."
During an interview with Congress of Racial Equality's (CORE)
National Spokesman Niger Innis, MSNBC displays a graphic
identifying him as "Nigger Innis."
Not even the best urban legends can surpass true stories like the
ones above. You can't make that stuff up.
Well, yea you can. You just have to bill more per word.

There is a white short bus that comes and picks up the residents
of Sunny Vale Assisted Living every Wednesday.
Those that still have their faculties about them walk onto the
thing and go grocery shopping. Some bring along their own bags.
Colostomy bags, ileostomy bags. My father is not one of them.
He is not allowed to leave the campus. The room, even. Not
without an orderly. Assisted leaving.
"Here ya go, pops."
That's Benny as me. He hands my father a vacuum-sealed pack of
sliced ham and a Kosher pickle wrapped in white paper. I've
never called him pops.
"He won't remember anyway, Dude."

Three hundred and fifty dollars. In travellers' cheques. That's how
it's spelled. American Express. That's what Benny gets from my
father this time around. Benny as me. Me as my father's
accountant. Benny as the Roto-Rooter man. Me as my father's
physician. His Lithuanian cousin. Last month we got two
hundred. All Benny wants is a slice of pepperoni and anchovies.
Large Mountain Dew and garlic sticks. The rest is acting chops.
Training ground.
"Pocket, Dude. Gotta have pocket."

The problem is they're going to amputate my father's foot. The
other problem is, he needs a new liver.

The Corporate Angel Network, an organization that coordinates free air travel for cancer patients, began when Coca-Cola executives arranged for the Blue Angels to fly a liver from San Diego to Houston in time for a transplant into a little girl.

My most popular story was the one about the home video showing an attractive, scantily clad woman licking under the rim of the toilet at an extended-stay hotel in the South, demonstrating how clean their apartment homes were.

That was unclassifiable veracity, which somehow turned legend. The ridiculousness of truth is unsurpassed.

See also: honesty.
See also: pathological displacement of erotic interest and satisfaction to a fetish.
See also: advertising for Extended Stay U.S.A.

Benny says, "Yea Dude I bet every guy ran home to get off on that one." And then he gives me the travellers' cheques.
"Checks, Dude."
That's how it's spelled.

(pt. 6)

The thing is, they can't be too long. These stupid stories. They can't go on forever, otherwise people stop reading. Believing. And so I need to find a way to end it.
"I know how, Dude."
We need to find a way to end it.
Benny says: "We off your old man, Dude."
Trite but...
"It's Hollywood, Dude. It's what they want. The *denouement*."
I say, "How do you know that word."

And Benny makes the double-guns with his thumbs and forefingers and does that chack-chack noise with his mouth and tongue.

See also: Isaac the Bartender.

"We off your old man with a pillow."

"And then what?"

"He leaves you all his shit. His homes, cars. He leaves all that to you."

Trite but…definitely Hollywood. And there has to be a kicker, too. A set-up for a possible second part, if this does well at the box office.

Benny says: "There's a detective who…"

Only this time I don't follow the two conversations. Just mine. Benny's tale spins out like a screenwriter's paradise. Twists and turns down Sunset. Hollywood archetypes.

I'm on to the new one. The one about the two guys who work at a major troubleshooting call-in center and go around wealthy neighborhoods at night, drinking the bait beer out of people's slug traps.

"That's sick, Dude."

Maybe, but those kinds are the best. I ask Benny if he thinks I'm a good guy. Overall, I mean.

"No way, Dude. You're an asshole."

And he's right. But it's how I get off.

"What kind of beer is it, Dude?"

It's a wealthy subdivision so it's imported stuff. So it gets you drunk quicker.

See also: Tuborg.

See also: Stella Artois.

See also: The Slug-X Trap.

"Kick ass, Dude."

Everything is a story. For the good ones, you just charge more per word.

4th Week in Rehab
(Bong Is Bard, February 2012)

Fuck.

Fuck. Fuck. Fuck.

Every place is the same. Fucking fuck.

God. He's everywhere. Here. Before. Before that. And sixteen times before that.

Fuck.

It's like nothing can be done without God.

god.

They have no faith in anyone in these facilities. Why am I here. Why am I here.

?

Hey man.

(a large black woman with a hair net)

You ok?

I don't know.

Fucking God.

God bless you, she says and leaves.

And all I want is a drink. Anything. Vodka. Gin. Bourbon. Grain. Grain. 180 proof.

They come in and out of my life in here, slide in and out, like transients. And they all spew the same old jive. God this. God that. Carrying little printed Bibles.

Fuck God.

God left a long time ago, you pitiful, spineless fucks. There's no one here. We're all alone. God hasn't been here in millennia.

She comes and touches my cheek. She looks down in between my legs.

Alexandra.

She says she's devoted her life to God and to the Twelve Steps and that each day is better than the last.

Another one.

Good luck lady.

But I still want to fuck her.

What did you say? She says.

I don't know.
What?
What did you say? Just now.
I don't know. Nothing.
Are you all right?
No.
Are they giving you meds?
Librium and...

in florida one morning high on meth i spotted a krispy kreme
truck instead of going to work i followed the van all the way up
military trail from ft lauderdale to west palm beach hoping it
would lead me to the krispy kreme factory when instead it went to
a storage facility it was a private moving truck bought from the
franchise but not changed over to reflect its new status i lost my
job as a doorman in boca raton and afterwards i went to a bar
which served romanian visinata and got drunk on nearly one
gallon of it

...diazepam.
They're giving you diazepam?
Yes.
That's good. Have you found Jesus yet?
What?
Jesus. Have you found Him.
I don't know. Which annex is he staying in?
I laugh. My face hurts. My head feels as if it's in a vise.
She looks in between my legs again.
I want to fuck her. This Jesus freak. This Bible thumper. Is it
wrong? Is it sinful?
What?
I don't know, I say. Why?
She laughs. Why are you here?
I signed myself in.

Without Jesus you're nothing.

All right, He co-signed.

I still want to fuck her. More so now. I hate her. Alexandra. I hate these people who find meaning in all the wrong corners.

What's that on your cheek, she says.

A burn mark. I burned myself with a hot knife sharpener.

Why?

I don't know. I need the pain. To keep me from going insane.

She puts up her hand and makes a "stop" motion. And she shakes her head.

You don't want to help yourself; I can tell that, she says.

And leaves.

—

Mark is the ex-counselor who landed in here after a bad relapse in his garage. He was caught by his wife drinking vodka out of a milk jug painted black, which supposedly held a spare gallon of gasoline for his boat. Mark is a good guy. But he's also a God guy. He smokes incessantly. I like his voice. He's calm and settled. I guess that's what happens when you let Him into your heart. I don't know. I don't know about that. Mark snapped one afternoon during a counseling session with a sixteen-year-old goth girl in Tallahassee, Florida. She told him about being sodomized by her father with a toilet paper roll dispenser. She confided in him that she liked it. And that's when he closed down his practice. Mark is a good guy. He reads from his Bible every morning. He takes long breaths. He doesn't push anything on me. He has a nine-year-old daughter. He's divorced. His wife and kid live somewhere in Utah.

We're in Erie, Pennsylvania, I think.

I play cards with Mark. And backgammon. He lets me win at backgammon. I can tell. He makes one wrong move. I tell him about my grandfather.

He tells me about the house they renovated before his relapse in the garage.

He was a professional chef, before he had his practice. He met his wife at Florida State. They were both MSW candidates.

Double sixes, he says. Lucky man.

I move my pieces on points.

Mark is a nice man. He doesn't push God on me. But I can tell he doesn't understand how I live like this. Without anything. I can tell he doesn't understand how I can ever get better, without God. And it's all right; because I don't understand how he lives like he does either.

Wanna take a smoke break?

I say yes.

We go out. He lights his Salem. Then mine. We stand there. And don't say anything the entire time.

4th Week (Redux)

...and we're quiet for maybe twenty minutes. I am comfortable with that. So is Mark.

He opens up his small Bible and thumbs through to the middle. I wait for him to start. They're all salesmen in here.

God is an indispensable product.

But he doesn't say anything. He just reads to himself. And smokes.

The ceiling fan breaks up the blue vapor above us.

Where is this place? The land looks scarred from the weather. Beaten up. Defeated.

Where is this place?

I'm sorry? He looks up.

Where are we?

You don't know?

I'm not sure.

Harborcreek, he says. Just east of Erie.

I think: Lake Erie.

Pennsylvania. Erie, Pennsylvania. How long have you been here? He closes the small book.

A month maybe.

Who's your counselor?

Cody.

There's been no work the entire time I've been locked in. Blank sheets of paper. Stacks.

We sleep three to a room. The men snore. And fart.

I stuff toilet paper into my ear canals but the grinding gets through anyway. I'm not sure how long I'll be in. Not sure if I'm well or if I'll ever be well. Not sure who can get me out. Or if I sign myself free. They won't tell us anything. Just to get better. We're all getting better. War is Peace. Oceania has always been at war with Eastasia.

He's good. Cody. (Mark again.) He's a good man. He cares.

He has a mustache.

Mark laughs. I'm not sure why I say that. I'm not sure he's sure either. There's a long pause.

I think: here it comes. The Sales Pitch. ABC. Always Be Closing. Always Be Closing when they're wounded.

Up for some backgammon?

Sure, I say. You can't let me win, though.

Mark laughs.

I'm serious.

He makes me tell him about my grandfather. Again. I don't know why. But I tell him. It makes him happy. We roll. We move. We bump. We come back in on points. We smoke. A nurse comes in and pulls the thin, white drapes to shield the room from the winter sun. She picks up a tray with discarded, dirty dishes. We roll. And we move. And I tell Mark how my grandfather slaughtered the pig at Christmas time in the old country and how he made sausages and boiled the kidneys and served them with salt and pepper and horseradish.

Nth Week in Rehab
(Amphibi.us, February 2010 / Bong Is Bard, March 2012)

i'll tell you this.
the last time i burned rock in the glass dick
they found me in a santa suit walking up and down Military Trail
throwing bags of shit at cars and reciting Kierkegaard outloud.
i woke up in the drunk tank
in hallandale beach florida
next to a cuban tranny
who was urinating in my hair entertaining the other men.
over here
the addiction you have
is replaced with the addiction to God.
The Twelve Steps.
a higher power.
i don't know what's worse
living in the suburbs paying bills and clocking in and out of a state
job
mowing your lawn every friday
taking the kids and wife to the mall
snapping family portraits and sending them to grandma
or putting in a 12-hour shift on the kill floor of an abattoir
taking hits of whiskey during breaks
or smoking meth at happy hour.

("oh how men suffer for children.")

The Informer

Metzger comes in smoking a clove.

He says, "I need to hit the head."

Marco is sitting on the torn fabric couch reading *How To Communicate Effectively Using Tact and Respect.*

"Hit the what?"

"The head. The bathroom."

Marco says, "The head." And snorts.

"It's an ancient navy term. It's named after the holes in the bow of old sailing ships. You know, the ones that had hammocks instead of bunks?"

"Yea. Don't splash piss all over the floor though."

"I know."

"And don't fuck with the kid in there."

Metzger steps into the mildewy washroom and unbuttons his pants. He holds the clove in between his lips. At the corner of the mouth. While he pisses, he leans laterally from the waist and looks at himself in the small mirror above the sink. He drags. The ashes light up for a second. And disintegrate on their way down to the dirty tile. Metzger turns his head. The kid looks like a teenager. He's hogtied in the bathtub with his shorts around his ankles. There's a thick river of dried blood leading down from his rectum to the back of his right thigh. Some of the blood has coagulated into dark red sticky balls along the way.

Marco says, "Don't splash."

"I got it. Jesus motherfuck."

Marco says, "Animal," and looks into the bathroom, over his book cover.

Metzger finishes. He pulls tightly on the belt. The leather bunches up his pants like a hobo's. He steps over to the kid and looks at his high tops.

"These the new Air 23s?"

The kid shivers and nods. His mouth is held shut with silver, contractor grade duct tape.

"Nice going, you. How'd you get these?"

And then back to Marco, "My man's got the 23s. D'ja know that?"

"What'd I say about fucking with the kid?"

"No, I'm just looking."

Marco says, "They're not my size anyway."

"Can I take them?"

Marco says, "Did you splash?"

"No."

"Don't let me step in any puddles you dirty pig."

"Jesus fucking Christ."

"Again, you savage. Leave him there. Don't take anything off a him."

Metzger comes down the hallway. He leaves flexible circles of smoke behind him. Marco looks at him over the book. Then goes back to his page.

"How much they owe you?" Metzger says. Then, "You got any barbecue chips?"

"No. I don't have chips."

"How much they owe you?"

"What difference does that make?"

Metzger says, "I'm just trying to make conversation."

Marco doesn't answer.

"Seriously, how much do they owe you?"

"Six-fifty, Jesus Christ. He doesn't stop, this guy."

"Oh yea? Six-fifty, heh?"

Marco says, "Yea, six-fucking-fifty. Heh."

"Listen, you hear about Viagra curing jetlag?"

Marco snorts.

"Yea. Some Argentine doctors found that Viagra helped hamsters recover up to fifty percent faster from forward shifts in time cycles."

"Oh yea."

"Yea but. See, the drug only worked in conjunction with light therapy. And only in one time direction. The equivalent of flying eastbound."

Marco says, "That's fascinating you useless freak. You got something for me?"

Metzger throws down a roll of twenties and some ones. Marco goes back to his book.

How To Communicate Effectively Using Tact and Respect.

"You gonna keep the kid until, what. Mama pays up?"

Marco says, "Are we done here then."

Metzger pats himself down for another cigarette. "Yea, yea."

"When you leave, pull up on the door so it latches. If you don't, it won't latch properly."

Metzger looks down the hallway into the bathroom. He pats himself again. He nods and makes a crooked face.

"Are we fucking done here, then for fuck's sakes."

Marco says that while he turns the page and rubs it between his fingers.

"Yea. Yea, oh yea."

Metzger grabs the doorknob and twists left first. Then right. He goes through. He shuts it behind him. The door clicks back open.

"Pull up so it latches."

"I know. I got it."

Kid
(In Other Words: Mérida, March 2012)

nobody calls me that no more.
just the old timer.
nobody calls him that either. old timer.
kid.
now look…no…don't. kid, don't.
that's how he talks.
don't, lookit. you gotta baste the dough with the egg mixture first before you put it into the oven. glaze it. and then sprinkle the salt bits so's they gets baked on there and stick. the salt. sprinkle the salt now, kid. atta boy.
nobody says that no more.
atta boy.

I think i'm living in the funny papers.
so long now, see you in the funny papers.
nobody says that.

i wake up early on sundays.
earlier than my parents, who sleep on a pullout in the living room.
someone stole our car.
i deliver the sunday newspaper.
the plain dealer.
the free times.
the news daily.
the stater.
bake at three se-nty fi for twenny minutes.
before i leave i put the tray into the oven.
i've made them pretzels.
pretzels for breakfast.
nobody has that.
nobody has what i eat for breakfast either.
green onion with salt, radishes, and a cup of mint tea.

hey kid, where can i take me the RTA Paratransit?
where you going? stadium? flats east? parmatown mall? where?

any of them.

take the 67AX or the e-line trolley. switch over to the 20A or the 23 for parmatown.

jesus, kid, watch the time on those things. you're gonna burn them. how long they been in there?

i walk back into the kitchen at the end of my shift with two bottles of champagne.

someone clipped them and left them in the trash room.

and i stole them a second time.

i sit down and sear tilapia in a cast iron pan.

pour the fizzy drink into a green glass jar.

i can hear my grandfather scream through a layer of putrid generations:

kid, lemme make you a fillet of...

Orange Cigarettes
(Specter Literary Magazine, November 2011)

Are you twenty-five feet from the building?

An old short man with a wide sun hat made from straw and a conference participant bag of goodies clutched to his chest.

I pretend I don't hear him but I spy him through my dark glasses not turning my head to make it look like I'm unaware. He doesn't even exist. I've been hassled for smoking too close to a federal building before. And always by old men and women who attend continuing education classes inside. They all smell like warm death and are probably all ex-smokers given the geography and the history of this land. Hypocrites. I've dealt with them all. Promiscuous girl turns Bible thumping born again virgin with a locked chastity belt. That kind of shit walking around is a dime a dozen. I despise taking lessons from the elderly. They never really give anything worth your while anyway. Nothing good you can take from the elderly. Not this elderly. Just their opinionated conservative bile and judgment. Once I called a lady with a walker Judgy McJudge for passing me by outside in the courtyard and offering up a contemptuous Mhhhpf as I blew the grey smoke away from her.

Are you twenty-five feet from the building? Young man?

I'm not young.

He laughs.

Well?

Well what?

Are you twenty-five feet from the building?

I look back at the wall.

Seems about right.

Good. Cause they're real sons a bitches about it since they put the law into effect.

He reaches into his breast pocket and pulls out a long orange pack of Pall Malls. In relation to his petite stature the 100s look like drumsticks hanging out from in between his lips.

One day I'm gonna quit he says.

But not today.

He laughs.

Well hell he says I'm no quitter. Never been that sort.

We're all trying I say.

I been trying since I was fourteen he laughs. Back then packs were twelve cents.

Jesus.

Right. You see how much they charge in New York City I say.

Ten bucks.

Ten bucks.

Still though he says. I'd like to quit. I'm seventy-eight years old. Doctor says I gotta quit.

Yea. We're all trying. But some of us got more than one weak side.

He likes that one. Course it's always gonna be something he says. Food drink stress.

A bus.

He laughs: true.

There's a risk outside your door every day I say.

That's it. My brother in law got lung cancer from working at a print shop all his life. Never once smoked.

Chemicals?

I guess so he says. Toner and ink and all that.

And then there was Andy Kaufman I say. Same thing. Never once smoked. Lung cancer.

Who's that?

Comedian. Was.

Always something he says. Babies got to sleep on their bellies. Then on their backs. Then on their bellies again. What's it now?

I don't know I say. They flip flop.

He laughs.

Doctors I mean. They flip flop every other year it seems.

Doctors he says.

Nobody knows anything about anything really I say. My kid's got seizures and they can't find anything. So they gave her a pill to take every day for two years. Nobody knows anything about anything.

He takes a drag and a long pause. And says: and that's the best thing I've heard in a long time young man.

I'm not so young. Forty-two next month.

Yea maybe.

I laugh. He drags. I drag. He clutches the bag of goodies tighter to his chest.

I gotta get inside he says. They're giving me a CAB.

What's that?

Combat Action Badge.

Really.

Yea. The Army. Korea.

I'll be damned.

I have no use for it he says. Doesn't matter. Only matters to them. Them ones that give it.

Isn't that how it always goes?

He laughs: you'll be surprised how many fellows care for these things.

I probably wouldn't.

He laughs: wouldn't care or wouldn't be surprised? Puts out his butt on the concrete but holds on to the extinguished burnt filter.

You want it?

Want what?

The badge. You want it?

I haven't served I say. Ever.

Maybe in your own way he says. I don't know. People serve in their own ways. Guarantee that.

Ah no I couldn't take that. Would make no sense.

Would make as much sense as them giving it to me.

No it wouldn't.

Make you a deal he says. If you're out here when they let me out you can have it.

He moves toward the glass double doors of the building and discards the crushed cigarette butt into the container next to the newspaper machine. I watch him go into the lobby through foggy glass. Before he blends into the sea of elderly veterans, I see him take off his hat and pat down his thin hair.

A Brief, Weird History of John 3:16
(On Barcelona, May 2012)

Myron Sobiesky always hated sports. I can tell you that for sure. He and I went to Taft Elementary and Emerson Middle in Erie, Pennsylvania so I knew him really well. We also hung out with Cory Boland—you probably remember him from spiking Tylenol bottles with cyanide in Chicago in 1982—but at the time Myron moved out to Spokane, Cory was still small time; doing a few months in Juvie for clipping Mrs. DiNardo's Ford LTD from a Revco parking lot. I didn't hear anything about Myron until some weird letter came in my parents' name fifteen years later saying how he had found the Lord through some guy on TV, had been reborn, and saved. It also said to watch the first game of the '77 NBA finals to see how he was spreading the Lord's word. Portland played Philly that year, and I wasn't much into b-ball, but I watched and I saw him wearing a rainbow colored afro wig and holding a sign up with "John 3:16." I had no idea what in hell that meant, but they kept showing him for some reason. After that, he'd pop up at any major sporting event that was televised. He was everywhere. Behind NFL goalposts, near Olympic medal stands, and he even got into the Masters at Augusta National Golf Club, standing strategically with his sign behind key shots of plays or athletes. John 3:16. I never understood what that meant. I wasn't a big fan of any religion. Actually, to this day I've never read the Bible. All that I know is junk I've heard from people trying to get me to go to church. Anyway. Myron. He became famous for his stunts. A weird sort of pop culture star from the 70s and 80s. As far as I know, he had no other occupation. He did nothing else.

In 1980 he was jailed briefly in Moscow at the Olympics. I remember we were boycotting the Games that year because of the Soviets invading Afghanistan, but somehow Myron made it over there with his damned signs. John 3:16. Mishka the Bear was the mascot, and there's a picture the Washington Post ran that summer with Myron standing behind that stupid bear in a T-shirt that said "God Thinks This Stinks." That must've been the start to some other weird phase, because after Moscow, Myron started setting off stink bombs back in the States. He got Robert Schuller's Crystal Cathedral, The Orange County Register, the Trinity Broadcasting Network, and some Christian bookstore. "God Thinks This Stinks."

In '92 I was out in L.A. working in a toy factory in Reseda on Wilbur and Saticoy, where the center of the Northridge earthquake was later, when Myron got into a standoff with police at a Holiday Inn Express in Lawndale. It was all over the national news. He and a couple of his buddies forced themselves into a room and tried to kidnap a maid, who ran and locked herself into the bathroom. Myron started yelling some junk about the Rapture coming in six days. During the standoff, he threatened to shoot down airplanes taking off from nearby LAX and covered the hotel windows with John 3:16 placards.

That was it.

That was the end of it all. That fast.

Myron Sobiesky is currently serving three life sentences on kidnapping charges. He was eligible for parole in '02 but was denied. He was denied again in '05. Up until then, Myron ran a blog, but I never read any of it. What I know is, his mother died in a house fire in 1966, and shortly after that his sister was murdered in a botched robbery in Missoula. He got married in 1986 and was divorced four years later. I think he had a kid, but I'm not sure. Might've been a little girl.

By the way, I finally looked up chapter three, verse sixteen of the Gospel of John. It says: "For God so loved the world, that he gave his only begotten Son, that whosoever believeth in him should not perish, but have everlasting life."

This is also printed on cups at the In-N-Out Burger.

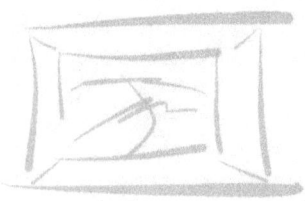

I Kant

How I feel is, I'm a fresh aphthous ulcer being doused in pure lime juice.

How I feel is.

Remember? Conversion engine. Surface breadth. Great circle distances between cities.

Here to Rabat: 4222.08 miles

Here to Damascus: 5656.73 miles

Here to Quito: 2323.03 miles

Here to Toronto: 798 miles. On Tuesdays and Thursdays. But on Fridays, Mondays, and Sundays it's 813 miles. Remember? I can't.

Mercopress:

"Falkland Islands hydrocarbons exploration development and the potential to hire a rig for a minimum six-well drilling program advanced considerably on Monday when Desire Petroleum announced that it had accepted the terms of an offer to farm in to three of the company's eighteen exploration prospects in the North Falkland basin."

Between Abu Dhabi and Accra: 3811.7 miles. Thirty-three twelve nautical.

Between Albuquerque and Algiers: 5721.1 miles. Forty-nine seventy-one nautical.

Here to here:

Thirty-three miles. Still un-calibrated. Between here and here, great circle: 33 miles.

It comes up over and over.

Latitude: 38°:49m 0s N

I also enjoy immobilization, etymology, and tickling.

Again. My own coordinates.

33.

Thirty-three.

Three-three with a red asterisk in the form of a hyperlink. It's a Wikipedia entry for "Hades."

Also known as Pluto. The unseen one.
Here to Pluto: 2.7 billion miles. Roughly.

Though our knowledge begins with experience, it does not follow that it arises out of experience.
I am trying to follow this while sirens are blaring outside my window for the third time to-day. Fire trucks and EMS at the Our Lady of Perpetual Sorrow Assisted Living Facility. It's the third heart attack of the day. Three and you're out.
"Though our knowledge begins with experience, it does not follow that it arises out of experience."
I am trying to follow this.
I Kant.

Picking Teeth in the Confessional Booth

Do not for a minute think I see myself as a pariah. Nor am I a martyr for doing this. After all, the only difference between suicide and martyrdom is adequate press coverage. The only reason I'm dictating all this into a machine is so the State can properly wrap up its case and pay out what families deserve.

One-e-and-uh, Two-e-and-uh, Three-e-and-uh, Four.

Everything's mapped out in the daily planner on the counter. At eight o'clock I am supposed to oil the wood floors. At nine-thirty, dust the counters. Twelve, pull weeds. Pull weeds. Spray poison. Stuart.
He's the new Cube.
He's got his framed pictures of his wife and kid all over the linoleum-covered desk. Brita pitcher. Fancy espresso machine with a network of thin tubes, 63 mm. grinder burrs, and faint yellow, dried membrane of milk froth around the cam stopper spring.
He's a gluttonous, weird, savage man with crossed pupils and red hair cropped close and perfectly uniform, like a helmet.
Like a porcine porcupine.
His office is extruded straight out of a Pottery Barn catalogue. Scented candles.
A smooth clock crafted to look old fashioned, made of pewter.

I had a friend in Harrare who committed suicide by eating dirt. She was a waif of a thing. She didn't stand a chance. There's a name for this: geophagy. Usually, soon after ingestion, an esophageal rupture will occur, then peritonitis, then in a few hours, death. I was called to identify her body:
Beauty marks.
Moles remind me of cancer reminds me of parasites remind me of bumblebees.

One-e-and-uh, Two-e-and-uh, Three-e-and-uh, Four.

You count out 4/4 bars like that. For fills, you add the "e-and-uh" and do your roll. It's easy hitting synthetic skin while you count. How this feels is, I am just a task in God's daily planner. I'm wedged in between Ages of Reason, Bronze, Iron, Dark Ages, Renaissance, Age of Aquarius, Electronic Age, Enlightenment, and other history-defining jargon. With a little luck, in thirty years I'll be finished. Then another entry will be properly erased. Crossed out. Stressed out. Another natural death. An "ism."
"How ya doin'?"
Stuart.
He's the new Cube.

Glory Hole
(Manarchy Magazine, October 2012)

[slang] A hole in a wall through which fellatio or masturbation was originally conducted incognito between male homosexuals. Now more popular with heteros.

"Oh, brother. Oh, dear," she says.

It's the hole in the side of the cubic stall. It's whispering at me.

"What you need right now is a miracle," she says.

I say, how do you know?

"I have your script right here. That's how."

Because my analyst tells me there needs to be a romantic interest. Because without that there's no literary tension. That's what he says. It's either him or my agent. I don't remember anymore. And so here she is. My emotional unbalancing force. Squatting in the stall next to mine, in the men's bathroom on the 9th floor of the Rockefeller building. Squeezing her words through a warped, cylindrical perforation just above my right knee. The twenty-first century love of my life. This one transcends electronic mail and chat and mobile phones and text messaging and all that convoluted social fabric offered by the Internet in the form of friendly websites through which you can connect.Facebook.MySpace.eSpin.Flickr.Friendster.Orkut.Xanga. This one comes to me through an aperture in a public toilet. Unseen. A blind date. A blind love.

I say, what script? Prescription?

"No. Your script. Your paper script," she says and jams what looks like a teleplay, flat against the tiny opening.

"What you need is a miracle, yes?"

I say, what I need is a few Demerol and a handful of Valium.

"Shh. Whisper."

I say, what I need is an injection of *Botulinum* Toxin Type A into the forehead. And maybe right above the corners of the eyes. Crow's feet are a bitch when you're adored. Or about to hit martyrdom on live TV.

"Whisper."

I say, what I need is some prednisone.

Dexamethasone.

Triamcinolone.

"Shh."

Fludochortisone or some Vitamin D derivative. Steroids.

I say, what I need is that. Not some fleeting miracle.

I say, miracles are for the faithful.

"Oh dear," she whispers.

Someone walks into the washroom, clears his throat, spits into the sink, and takes the stall to my left. He drops his pants and lets go of the explosion. She stifles a laugh, then says: "Shhh."

How I feel is, I'm on horseback on my father's ranch in Del Rio inspecting a 15-mile stretch of the border fence and I come up on three Mexican Army soldiers standing on our side of the land balancing FX-05 Xiuhcoatl assault rifles on their shoulders.

"Shh."

How I feel is, when you take off the plastic wrap from a TV dinner after ten minutes of being zapped by electromagnetic waves and the steam burns holes into the delicate skin on the bottom of your wrist.

"Whisper."

The man finishes and cleans himself with toilet paper. The smell of his business is thick with every breath that goes into my lungs. I'm tired of smelling men's bowels. He pulls up his pants and steps out. He walks straight past the sinks without washing his hands. As he opens the door he pauses and throws back: "You fucking fairy faggots," before he lets the door slam.

She's right.

What I need now is a miracle.

I say, what's your name.

According To
(Jumping Blue Gods, December 2012)

(one)

Irritants.

For example. This book I'm reading. The font of the numbers at the bottom of the page. For example. It's bubbly and fat.

The font.

I don't know what you call it. Arial. Trebuchet. Courier. I don't know these things. Serif, sans serif. I shot the sheriff. Whatever. The font of these things makes them look like insects. When you're reading and you're seeing these numbers on the periphery, these bastards look like bugs. I'm telling you. Don't laugh. And if you move the pupils along with the text, and you do because you're reading for Chrissakes, they look like *moving* bugs. You know? You hold the thing in between your thumb and forefinger...well, down in the crease between the digits, and the things are actuating. They're supplanting on the fucking page, these arthropods.

The zero is a tick.

The one is an ant.

The three is an aphid.

You get it. Every fifth line I feel like smacking down on the book. Listen, if you're reading this, stop. Do me a favour. Go find something else to distract you. There must be something on TV. Get a facial. A pedicure. Let those mousy Asian women draw minuscule flowers on your toenails. Color your hair. You look like shit, pushing forty. Your skin is flaky. Drink some water.

Don't start in on this. I'm warning you, you'll just get pissed off. What this is, is just another confession of a lousy, anonymous sap. An addict. A twelve-stepper. Nothing new. We're a dozen a dozen. Even I'm sick of it.

Step 4: Make a searching and fearless moral inventory of yourself.

Step 4.

The four is a twisted silverfish.

I'm serious. Don't waste your time reading this. You won't find anything good here.

Stop.

(two)

Fine.

Go.

Where am I?

Irritants.

Like people who say "anyways" or "Febyooary" or "nukular" or "supposebly" or "irregardless" or "as per" or "a myriad." I once sat in on a meeting in which the big honcho kept talking about another CEO's rolodex, and it didn't become clear until a few minutes in, that our man was actually referring to his counterpart's Rolex timepiece.

Irritants.

Like lye on skin. Poison oak. Small talk.

What I'm addicted to is being addicted. Or, rather, getting help for being addicted. Only I'm not addicted to any particular vice, nor am I visibly ravaged by a degenerative disease. I'll take anything they have available for that night: Support for men with prostate cancer, survivors of mesothelioma, N-stage breast cancer patients (men develop a rare form of breast cancer usually in their 60s or 70s, but I'm always the rare case, which gets more attention and more pity), thyroid problems, leukemia, parents of children with brain tumors.

Anything.

Television, even though I don't own one. Internet porn.

Electronic mail. Depression. Bi-polar support. There's a feel-good group for everything out there, you just have to scour the back of the Independent and find your drug.

Child abuse.

I'm good with that. I know a bit about that. I know a bit about being the recipient of that, is what I mean. I used to think the physical was much easier to take than the mental. It's much more clear-cut. It's easier to forgive black and blue and purple bruises on the thighs and arms. The pain of it all is finding good excuses for the tracks. There aren't any. People know. But you give it to them anyway.

AnywayS (extra "S").

Irritants.

You do. You run into armoires, walls, you bump into nightstands, fall down the stairs.

Conveniently.

What happens over the decades with physical abuse is, it turns into the animal that eats at the inside of your brain. It morphs into the mental. So now you have two issues. Don't ask me how those things transform into sexual addiction or what they call deviance. It's why I go to these lousy meetings at night. To listen to how they figure it. Because I have no idea how you go from a leather belt on your back at age seven, to sleeping with a man twice your age in your parents' bed, while they're frolicking around Prague, drinking Pilsner Urquell and chomping on giant radishes.

Don't ask me.

(three)

Four nights a week I volunteer at a hospice just outside the demarcation line of the city. Our Lady of Perpetual Sorrow. That's not really the name; it's what I like to call it. The place is off Florida Avenue. You know it. That brown, asbestos infested edifice down by the fish market where the Italian guy slices off capicolla and pancetta with a rusty knife, and wraps baccala in newspaper. All the while screaming at you: *ma vafangu you lousy gagootz*! It's atrocious watching people wither away to nothing. But it's also a type of addiction. My addiction: observing death take over a complex system. They don't have support groups for that. That's why I go to the others. The cancers. The thyroids. The blood disorders. To see how they apply their twelve steps, and plagiarize. Or adapt. Or adjust. I live in other people's stories. Remember? A copy of a copy of a copy. I am an insomniac haunted by Kafka's Felice and her rotting teeth. You know Felice? She was his first love. Only he despised her teeth. And now, so do I. I live in his books. I live in his Castle.

yea gimme a Manhattan, add bitters.

I've seen people being decapitated with dull knives, or being tied up and shot in the head, or thrown off buildings handcuffed, landing on their necks or spines. Or in Uganda: men and women with their limbs cut off and sewed back on, but reversed. You ever wanna know what it looks like to have legs for arms and arms for legs? Come have a few drinks with me. And don't call me a boy. I'm not a boy.

Forget it. Don't ask me about it. I told you, it's an addiction. It makes my insides turn and I can barely hold dry toast. But I go back and relive that. Over and over, I go back. With no support group.

Tonight I empty bedpans.

They still have those. I pissed in a yellow, plastic one when I was a child and lived in a two-room apartment on the eighth floor of the C.P.R. building in a cold, drafty city.

have I told you about the time I waved to Nixon's motorcade from the red room window of our apartment? remind me one day.

And turning them over to change the bedding. That's my task tonight. Bob Rothstein shits himself, and here I am with a suitcase full of cloth towels and soap and water. Upsidaisy old man. I turn him over and wipe off the dried excrement from around his cheeks and bottom of his thighs. I once studied to be an LPN. Licensed Practical Nurse. It didn't work out so well. They gave me the day shift and I couldn't step out into the morning. That was the year I spent living in my car. The trick is to find a parking

lot, which has long, pole, lights with concrete bases and A/C
outlets built into them. That was the year my parents are buried.
yea I know I'm switching tenses. are you paying attention?
After that, I studied to be a pharmacist. And then a pilot. My
friend passed on a copy of the DSM and I became addicted to
being addicted. I cleaned people's apartments for three years. It's
amazing the number of dildos I found stashed under mattresses,
or the amount of pornography stacked on the DVD player. I
became addicted to that, too. Pornography. Only that lasted a few
months. There's only so much you can do. So many holes you can
stick body parts into. And I'm not into pigs or donkeys or dogs,
although in Amsterdam I paid to watch a leggy blonde go down
on a horse.
Don't ask me about that. It turns my stomach. I cannot even hold
toast. I got off pornography one day. I just stopped watching.
That's how it was for cigarettes, too. One morning I woke up and
just had coffee. Twenty-two years of smoking just off the bed. I
got off it. Don't ask me how. I don't know anything about
anything anymore.
*remind me to tell you about a girl named Tramby who came and turned
everything upside down for me during a long winter in which i contemplated
going out with a Luger.*
Yea.
Remind me.
Because I lost my heart. I buried it somewhere. And she saved
me.

(four)

One way to do it is begging. Stealing works too. I never went for
any of that. Too much work. And theft doesn't quite mesh with
even my skewed definition of virtues. I got into medical trials,
sleep deprivation studies, control groups, double-blind

experiments, natural experiments, observational studies, field experiments, even a bizarre human vivisection trial based on my history and propensity for cutting my own flesh during high stress times, or suicidal and depression bouts. There is money in all that. And in plasma, too. You know plasma. The liquid part of your blood. Yellowish in color. Comprised of water and protein. Carries hormones and vitamins throughout your body. Red and white blood cells, and platelets are all suspended in plasma so they can circulate. Hemophiliacs need it because it helps with coagulation. Plasma products are also used to assist burn victims. So you see, it's ethical to get paid for it. You're helping people. But you're laughing at my skewed definition of ethics and altruism.

Plasma.

Twice a week I donated it. Since I'd been tested for Hepatitis B, and didn't have it, I'd get $60 a pop. Hundred and twenty a week. Do the math. Almost five C-notes a month.

Plasma is collected through a process called "plasmapheresis." When you come in to donate, a needle is placed in your vein and your blood is pumped into a specialized spinning device that separates the plasma from the other whole blood components, such as red and white blood cells and platelets. While the plasma is collected, the other blood components are filtered into a reservoir. Once the reservoir is full, your red and white blood cells and platelets are returned to your body. Throughout the process, the system automatically alternates between collection and replacement until the predetermined amount of plasma, based on your weight, is obtained. The tubing and all other collection supplies that come in contact with your blood are discarded and replaced with new, sterile materials each time a donation procedure is performed.

You have to eat something beforehand. And even throughout. Sometimes it takes eight hours for the shitheads to process you, identify you, test for HIV and other junk, and finally suck out the juice.

I got into selling plasma from living with my old man. He was a vampire for a time in the late '70s. He extracted plasma from drug addicts in Elyria. He got pricked so many times by used needles, his fingers and palms looked like a kid had gone berserk with a red pen on his flesh. But he never caught anything. My old man was a horse. When I was young, I thought he'd live forever. Anyway. Plasma. You have to be at least 110 lbs. in weight. Eighteen years of age.

And if you're a woman at these centers, any kind of a woman, expect to get hit on by the most decrepit swine parasites that ever walked the earth.

Only I'm not a woman.

We Don't Do Takeout
(Girls With Insurance, July 2011)

"I come from stock tainted with anachronistic philosophical ideas," he crowed from behind the decrepit, blackened stove while flipping a giant pancake with blueberries embedded in its still watery, raw batter. "See this? Some fucking stockbroker who's about to go on with his day sodomizing the hell out of all of us is gonna eat this little magnificent creation in about ten minutes."

He pointed to the griddle with his giant head. Sweat beads had formed on his forehead and temples.

"And after he's finished fucking everybody up the ass, he'll go home to his girlfriend and give her a Dirty Sanchez. A taste of the bourgeoisie, you see."

He laughed at his own lewd metaphor and flipped the pancake one more time.

"Watch…you wanna see how I get the glaze on it? Watch this."

He poured sugar on top of the pancake. To the side closest to his left arm, he had placed a steel spatula into the fire of his largest burner. The utensil had started to turn red from the heat.

"Here you go…"

He removed the spatula and ran it smoothly across the sugared top of the pancake, creating a sweet, caramelized caul of sorts.

"Here's your usual mister shithead," he laughed. "You know I dropped everything I ever owned in the stock market." He wiped the beads of salty sweat about to drop onto the hot griddle with his sleeve. "It was stupidity. My own fault. My kids hassled me not to do it. It's what happens when you're stubborn and stupid."

The orders came in. His daughter yelled back through the rectangular space separating the small eating area and the kitchen.

"Dad, come on."

"She takes this shit way too seriously," he laughed. "Pearl, relax! Baby. It's only food."

"Stuff it."

"She really does. She's like a komandant, you know."

The orders came in from Pearl, fired out of a verbal Tommy gun in a way that only lifelong Brooklynites can deliver.

"I love him," said one of the regulars—a man with a bushy beard, round spectacles, and baseball hat. "I've been eating here for thirty-two years. Best food in the city. Great portions. He's an institution, you know. Zagat digs him. And you always stand the chance of getting kicked out for whichever reason he feels necessary. I love him. He's terrifying. You never know what he's gonna do. He's walking behind me, isn't he?"

—

In August, three men with shotguns entered Sheindlin's and robbed the restaurant in plain view of customers, passersby, kids. Kenny Sheindlin's daughter was shot in the head as an afterthought, as the robbers were exiting. The story ran in the New York Post and later even made the Times in the form of a long profile on the little dive Kenny Sheindlin and his family ran for over thirty years.

—

The phone rings. He throws the spatula into the iron sink. He picks up and cradles the receiver in between his left ear and shoulder.

"Yea. No. No, we don't serve parties of five. It's the rules. Yea, well it's *our* rules. No, you cannot split off into a party of three and a party of two. You're still a party of five, see? Yes. No, ma'am. One hundred years from now, one hundred blocks from here you'll still be a party of five. That's right. Aha. What? No! We don't do takeout!"

He slams the receiver into its hook.

"Asshole."

Man Goes, Again
(Scissors and Spackle, June 2012)

He had just come up from Key West with a trunk full of mangoes. He talked like Bogart on meth.

"Twenny-four hours straight driving. You believe that? Twenny. *And* four. No stops. Ok, maybe two or three. Strictly to piss and gas up. Believe that? Only had one tape. Played the hell out of it...*Louder Than Bombs* by the Smiths. I never wanna hear Vicar in a Tutu again I'm telling you. Goddamned Morrissey. Never wanna hear that whiny ass voice ever again. I'm sick of it. All of it. Really. Although Marr is all right by me. Twenny-four hours straight. You get it. Want a drink? Make a mean daiquiri. Got enough fruit to last me a year. Ok maybe a month, the rate you and I down 'em. Old man has a mango tree out front. I tell you that? Last time he got pinched by...what's her name...what's her name? Come on. What's the last one that hit Key West? You know all that meteorological jazz."

"Wilma."

"Right, Wilma. *Wilmaaaaaa!* When was that?"

"Oh-Five."

"Right, Wilma, '05. Last time he got hit, my old man, damned hurricane straps gave out and the trailer was blown fifteen yards off the property. Believe that? Into the mango tree out front. Almost took it out, but didn't. Anyway. Got about forty pounds. Should last me a year. Ok, ok...a month. Wanna drink? Seriously." He chopped the concoction inside the blender and told tales of tagging marlin and sailfish out by Bimini with his father, Roddy, and his weird uncle.

"He kept trying to shove his thumb up my ass. Thought it was funny or something. Made a weird noise with his lips every time he tried to do it. You know how those country people are. Anyway. Next time you go out...you goin' down anytime soon? Well then, if you do go down, soon, next time...take the catamaran from in front of Jilly's downtown, out to Garden Key in the Tortugas. Go check out Fort Jefferson. Killer snorkeling, besides. Clown fish and all that goddamned tropical junk. Fort Jefferson, you get that? It was originally erected to be the largest fort in the coastal defense system during the Civil War, only the goddamn thing was never attacked and its value to coastal defense was rendered almost useless by the invention of the rifled cannon. After the Civil War, the fort served as a prison for who? For who? You know?"

"For whom."

"For? Bueller? Bueller? Voodoo Economics. I love that guy. You know that guy? The red eyes guy. You know him?"

"Ben Stein."

"That his name?"

"Yeah. He was a speechwriter for Nixon."

"Nixon?"

"Yeah."

"Goddamned rat. Haldeman and that entire crooked crew. No. Seriously. Fort Jefferson. It was a prison for Dr. Samuel A. Mudd. You know him?"

"Yeah. That was the guy who set the broken leg of James Wilkes Booth."

"Christ, I can never stump you. Assassin extraordinaire of senor President Love Daddy Lincoln, yes. Binga-roni, Trebek! Always knew you had it in ya. Gotta figure out the buzzer though. You know, that's the key. You know that, right? I mean everybody knows those goddamned questions. Answers. Whatever. It's the buzzer that's the bitch. Too early, it locks you out. Too late...well then...too late." He chopped up more fruit and went on about Martin, the Haitian doorman downstairs, and how he foiled a DEA bust of some apartment on the 15th floor, by calling up the residents and announcing the imminent "jackbooted fascist bumrush."

"Black helicopters and all that jazz my brother. For what? For what. Seriously. For a goddamned few ounces of doobie. I'm serious. In the name of Jaja. I swear...Marley must be turning in his grave."

Sometime around daybreak he disappeared into the other room to fetch another bottle of Myer's Rum. He was going on about the last one that hit the Keys in '30 and how it missed Hemingway by *this* much.

"By how much?"

"Oh, I see," he said. "When's your next gig at The Comedy Store?"

"No, I just want to literally see by how much Hemingway missed the storm."

"Listen," he said while twisting open the cap, "if you'd spent half the time in school you do busting my balls, you'd have been one of those JPMorgan CEO types."

"Hardly. Finance isn't in me."

"Yea, no shit. But listen, so what happens is, apparently the DEA gets word these saps on the fifteenth floor are running pills or E or K or whatever. You know what I'm saying. I mean these guys are just regular ol' rastamen...Jaja's disciples. You know Jaja, right? Jehovah? Yeah. Dreadlocks and doobies. No woman no cry. Redemption song and all that. You know the type. Peace-lovin' hippies, not dealers. So these government bozos come in dressed up all in black with riot gear and gats and all of it. Einsteins, right? Straight through the lobby, just like that. There's what...dozens of them. Something like that. You follow?"

"Yeah."

"They even take the goddamned elevator..."

"Dozens of them? In one elevator?"

"You know what I mean. They secured multiple lifts. Or they went halfsies and the rookies ended up taking the stairs. Whatever. Go figure it. Point is, these jackbooted Nazis make no effort to be subtle. Overt all the way, capish? Like a bull in a candy store."

"China shop."

"What?"

"Never mind."

"Right. Scare the shit out of the little ol' ladies hanging in the Amenities Center...in the lobby. And plus, it takes these goons a few minutes to trudge up all their gear and shit. But goddamned Martin the concierge calls up our boys from Jamya-ca mon, and literally announces that the Gestapo is on its way, so our boys have some time to flush stuff down toilets, or dump junk out the window. Can you see that? Ring ring, mothafuckas! Your guests, the SS, are on their way up. Meantime, I'm out here taking in some rays on the balcony and cataloging the last two weeks in the Keys, in my mind like. Right? Not to mention, I'm stressing because now I'm looking at literally forty pounds of mangoes I've got to somehow keep refrigerated. Anyway. So I'm out here and all of a sudden I see those righteous Rastafarians getting pushed up against the glass doors, inside the place, hands up, and all hell breaks loose. Soldiers come in, tear up the joint. Rip up carpets, knock things down, the whole nine...the whole enchilada, right? I'm out here like a fool watching it all go down thinking, Jesus...hunnerd bucks this shit ends up on the five-thirty with Maureen Bunyan."

"She still on channel seven?"

"Yeah. Listen, though. I mean I'm just kidding about this making the news. Think about it. This kind of shit never makes the broadcast. So, world war three is going down and suddenly, suddenly I think...catch this on video...you know...for my own pleasure and edification."

"Edification."

"Edification, you know...for my own uplifting information. *Enlightenment.*"

"I know what it means."

"Well then why'd you stop me? Anyway. I run inside, grab the thing, come back out and start shooting."

"Like a fool..."

"At's right. Like a goddamned buffoon. A saltimbanque."

"Saltimbanque! Christ, I'll be damned; you're an aristocrat."

"An aristoCAT. But listen, so I'm out here documenting, right? I mean, that's what I'm doing. Documenting."

"Sure."

"Right. So the goddamned slider door opens, and one of them...this bastard has on the helmet, black mask, baclava..."

"Balaclava."

"Yeah, I said that."

"You said baclava."

"Yeah."

"You mean balaclava."

"What the f... why do you keep interrupting? I said *baclava*."

"Never mind."

"Ok, so...yeah, semiautomatics, everything, right? It's the DEA. The goons. Gestapo tactics. Bells and whistles, fanfare pied piper the Yanks are coming. So this guy spots me getting all this on tape and says whatever he says into his little mic there, on his helmet? And points to me. Like points, but with impunity and aggression, you know? Like...like...uh! *Boom*. 'You goddamned agitator...'"

"He actually said that?"

"No, you shit...I'm...you know, embellishing..."

"Agitator?"

"Like, some jerk who stirs up public feelings on controversial issues."

"I know what it means."

"Well then...anyway, *Christ*. Stop laughing. Anyway. So yeah. No more than three minutes and two of these guys are knocking down my door talking about voyeurism, illegal wiretapping, infringement of rights...INFRINGEMENT OF RIGHTS! They say that. To me."

"Jesus."

"No kidding, right? I mean what? Really. I'm just some guy trying to figure out how I'm gonna get rid of my three boxes of mangoes. I'm just an informed citizen, right? An I-Reporter. You

know they have that? I-reporting? Where you shoot video of...
Anyway..."

And then he stops.

"Anyway what?"

"Nothing. What. Nothing. That's it."

"That's it?"

"Yeah. That's that. They took the camera and everything."

"That's it."

"Yeah. That's that. And there was nothin' I could do about it. And then here you are."

"Jesus that was pretty anti-climactic."

"What. *Life* is one big anti-climax, son. Deal with it. My real point here is that goddamned Martin...the goddamned concierge actually *announced* these guys up to the Rastafarians."

"Right. I got that."

"What I'm saying is, here's a guy who did his job. You know? That's it. A man committed to his craft. I mean, you gotta respect that, right? At least. At the very least."

"I wouldn't check the local papers on this one."

"Well that's what I said already. Hence the whole camera situation."

"Right."

"Chee-rist, you're a thick one. Not much for following conversation, are you."

"It's because you fizzled it at the end."

"I already said..."

"I know. Life's banal."

"And then you die. Don't you forget it."

"Now you're just one big cliché. All you need is some thick sideburns and an Isaac Afro."

"Fuck off," he said and readjusted something in between his legs. "...and stop laughing already."

"All right, all right. How's the baby?"

"He's fine. He's with his mother until next weekend."

"You ever going to take him down to meet his grandpa?"

"Maybe next summer. I don't know...I don't see this kid lasting more than two hours in a three hundred square foot trailer. He's a goddamned demolition squad, he is. It's gonna be brutal."

He went in to mix another round of drinks. I looked across to the west wing, into the raided apartment on the fifteenth floor. The blinds had been shut and ripped pieces of carpeting were stacked on the balcony along with some overturned chairs.

"We're out of rum," he yelled from the kitchen. "What now?"

"It's all right..."

"What's all right, you goddamned rummy. What is?"

I didn't answer. I didn't know.

My Agent

"What in fuck's name is ludefisk?"

"What?"

"Ludefisk, what is that?"

This is on the phone, in the throes of a massive hangover. Two days ago.

"What does that have to do with anything? What time is it? Am I paying for this call or you?"

"Oh yea," he says. "You're on Eastern time."

And he's not. He's in Veracruz. Actually, Alvarado. Still…that's three hours behind. That puts him around 2-something a.m. He's still up. The night before. It's today, the night before.

"Well?"

"Well what?"

"Ludefisk. What is that?" he says.

"Why do you ask?"

"It's in one of your stories. Have you given up, by the way?"

"What?"

"Smoking. Have you given it up?"

I hear him light up with a Zippo. To spite me, like.

"Piss off you cunt."

He laughs and coughs. And laughs phlegmatically like a donkey suffering from pertussis.

"Look it up."

"What?"

"Look up ludefisk," I say.

There's a long pause and a huge bang.

"What was that?"

A woman's voice. Irrational. Fighting. A struggle. He covers up the receiver and it all becomes muddled. Then:

"Ah, baby…"

Another bang. And:

"I can't look it up. She burned the dictionary."

"Jesus."

"And then she took a…what's that…the…one big hammer…"

"Sledgehammer."

"Yea. She took the hedgehammer and demolished my desk."

"SLEDGEhammer," I yell into the phone.

"Yea, yea."

"When was that?"

"Last week. We're all right now."

"Didn't sound like it. Is she gone?"

"No, not now now, just in general now. I mean, yea, she's gone. She said she'd come back to throw my typewriter out the window," he says.

"Jesus, heh? Special trip and all."

"Yes well…you know, she's fiery."

"And how."

"So then. Ludefisk?"

"Yea, I didn't know myself until some lady said…"

"Hold on, hold on, some guy is here with…"

Another bang.

"You all right?" I say.

"Hold on, this guy has a…" then he covers up the receiver but I still hear him:

"What is that? Wha? An X-ray…?"

And the line goes dead.

1977   **Mae**

We drove out to Pacific Palisades in his car—an orange Citroën—to pick up a rough-cut print of Total Recall.

You know last time I saw one of these was in '77 in Bucharest, I said.

Really? Commies liked something other than Volgas?

Shit Volgas. We had Ladas and Dacias 1300s. Trabants, too.

Jeesas, he laughed and coughed. Now that's some real donkey power right there. Hand me a clove, he said.

He lit it with a rusty Zippo.

Ever been to Santa Monica?

No. I just know it from Three's Company.

Shit, he laughed and coughed. That's good.

I punched buttons on the radio. It was an old radio. The kind that had hard buttons to depress. The type of buttons that would laboriously drag the tuner up or down the radio scale bar.

I ever tell you the story about how I got to photograph Mae West in the nude he said.

Jesus, really?

I get a call from Leo Dellabate, he said. Leo was the bandleader for Mae's Vegas show. He says to me he says you wanna take some pictures of Mae in the nude? He says that out of the blue. Believe that?

Jesus.

Jesus right. That's what I say. So...yea, I say to Leo. Come by the house Sunday at four Leo says. So? All right. I get the gear together and off I go. I get to the house and Leo opens the door. Says Mae's in her bedroom waiting. We go through...this was her house off the Pacific Coast Highway...you know it?

No.

Gorgeous thing. Anyway, we go through and Leo opens the fancy French doors to her...her *boudoir*, right? And there's Mae standing there in a bathrobe.

Good God.

And that's what I say. So I start setting up the gear, but she says to me she says not here. Over there. And she points to some atrium or salon or whatever in hell you call those open things with the plants and the water and all that. Okay I say and move the stuff over. We get there and there stands a goddamned marble statue of Mae West in the nude. She says to me I want you to photograph that statue, she says and gives me that smile. You know that smile?

I do.

So basically she tricks me. I ain't there to photograph Mae West in the nude, I'm there to photograph a nude statue of her.

Incredible.

Right? But still, she has a good laugh, Leo has a good laugh, we all have a good laugh, right?

I imagine.

Right. So I snap some shots but something don't look right. Okay so what? So I get Mae to lend me the goddamned statue to take to my house. I got this wonderful place in my garage, I tell her, I can put this thing against this beautiful green wall and photograph it. So she agrees.

She let you take the statue home?

Incredible right? But true. So me and Leo and a couple a guys from the band haul this goddamned thing over to my place. And I set it up against the nice green background in the garage...only something happens. I don't know what 'cause I have my back turned to it, you know? Getting the gear ready. But somehow....*somehow* the thing wasn't set right, right?

Oh shit.

Shit nothing. Worse. So just as I turn to face the thing and check lighting, I see it in slow motion like, you know? I see it tipping over toward me, coming down on its face but in slow motion, you know?

Right.

Boom, the thing falls just like that.

Oh shit.

But incredibly, only a finger breaks off. I mean...and...so anyway I scramble around trying to figure out what to do when Betty comes running into the garage and says: Marilyn Monroe is dead. She's...dead.

And so off we go.

Jesus. So what happened with the statue.

Well I found a body shop over on Reseda downtown that said they could fix it, so I got some of the fellas and we dragged the goddamned thing down there and they fixed it.

They fixed it?

Yup. And it was glorious I mean. Mae couldn't tell the difference.

Jesus.

Ain't that something, he said.

I swear you have the best stories.

Guess you stick around for long enough time you're bound to run into something good, he said.

Here it goes right here, I pointed out the windshield. He pulled on the wheel. The car squeaked into the turn.

Citroëns in goddamned Romania, he said. In nineteen-seventy-seven. I'll be goddamned.

It's a Princess' Life
(Blue Fifth Review – International Issue, July 2012)

Bermondsey.

I loved the name. I don't know if it's a real city. I read it in a book my dad gave me when I was just out of university.

Bermondsey. It could've been the name of our city. The Great City. It's a game Dad and I used to play when I was little. Maybe four or five. He'd lie down on the couch and I'd ride on his back to The Great City. He was the ship and I was the captain. I'd sail like that and he'd fall asleep for a few minutes. He'd give me hard candy when he'd wake up. Say he'd bought it from the gypsy vendors selling in the outdoor market on the docks of our Great City.

Later, when things were dark, he'd take me to the cinema on Saturdays. When I could get out of bed. He was a good dad. I never told him that. He was always there. Always. It was his turn, though. After all those years alone, it was his turn.

Bermondsey.

It was just stuck in my head all those years. It sounded nice and English. So proper. It sounded like somewhere where I belonged. In some other time, maybe. In a pub with some lasses. Fish and chips. And a warm fireplace on a dreary day. Maybe.

We had our rows, though. Dad and I. The night I came in after I broke my finger, when he took the bottle. That was our biggest row. He grabbed just below the twisty top and pulled it out of my hands. He was too strong. And I was trashed. My skin was itchy and blotchy around the neck. The drink always did that. I had eczema when I was little. Or psoriasis or something. The drink always made it come back. He took the bottle to the sink and emptied it. All of it. Perfectly good bottle of vodka. I had just bought it. Sixteen dollars. All of it down the drain. He had no right. Bloody fucking hypocrite. That's what I thought then. The rage came up from my belly. I grabbed his hair and pulled so hard, blood came out of his scalp. When it ripped it sounded like Velcro. There was blood trickling down his nose, into his mouth. It was awful. It was awful what I'd done. But I didn't care then.

He dumped a full bottle of vodka down the drain. That was more important. Then.

When I had my accident, he was there. Dad.

Daddy.

Da'.

I used to call him that, and he loved it. I used to do it in an Irish accent. Da'.

After I drove the Rabbit into the telephone pole. He was there. I broke my knee and my foot. After the impact, I ended up in the passenger seat. The police found me, and for a while they thought I was the passenger and the driver had bailed. It's what I told them. And they went looking for a drunk driver on foot. They went looking for a man who'd fled the scene. Only, I honestly didn't remember I was the driver. It's how soused I was.

"Dad?"

I didn't hear him on the other end. He must've just picked up and listened.

"Dad? Daddy?"

"Yes, love."

"Da'."

I didn't hear him. The room was too loud.

"Yes, love. I'm here. Livy. I'm here."

"Where?"

"I'm here. Coming to get you…Coming to get you?"

He'd said it twice, I thought. It sounded funny.

"Livy?"

"What?"

"Livy. Where are you, love? Livy? You called *me*. Let me come get you. Where are you? Love?"

"Bermondsey."

It was the only thing I could think of. It's where I wanted to be. The Great City.

I had cut my hand on something. Fuck. Broken glass.

I don't know how he found me. How he got there so quickly.

I vomited off the patio into the weeds. And then I fell into it.

He was always there for me. I just never told him. I should have. I loved him.

My Da'.

Loose Tooth

"Dad?"

"Yea."

"When your tooth fell out, did it hurt?"

"Hm?"

"When you lost your tooth. Did it hurt?"

The strangest thing is the dreams that come still. I get them. Frequently. Losing teeth and running my tongue over the open wound, still tasting the salty iron from the blood. I am a boy in these dreams, running after cars.

Trains.

Airplanes.

All of which are to take me home, but all of which leave without me.

Bloody gums. Missing my ride. A feeling of defeated incompetence mixed in with a hole in the chest.

Failure.

There is no God.

"My baby tooth?"

"Yea. Dad?"

"Yea."

"Did it hurt?"

"Why do you ask that? Did someone tell you it hurts when you lose a baby tooth?"

"Yea."

"Who?"

"Cooper."

"Is he old enough to have a missing tooth?"

"Dad?"

"Yea."

"Because I don't remember."

"What's that, Livvy?"

"I don't remember what it's like to lose a baby tooth."

"Are you asking *me* if I remember?"

I catch her in the rearview. Her face is concentrating on an invisible mark dotting the seat directly in front. She looks hypnotized.

"Livvy?"

"What."

"Do you mean to ask *me* if I remember what it's like to lose a baby tooth or are you saying *you* don't remember? Because you haven't yet lost one."

She cuts into the condensation on the inside of the passenger window with her index finger. She draws thick tree trunks that seem to melt away down into the panel of the door.

And then she giggles.

And giggles.

And stops:

"If there's blood, will you wipe it?"

"What blood?"

"From the tooth falling. Is there blood?"

"Usually."

"Will you wipe it?"

"Of course."

"With a wet tissue?"

"Or cloth. A cloth usually works better. Tissues leave little paper bits sticking to the...Even when wet."

She looks out at the land rushing by, through the foggy window. The condensation has glossed over her melting tree trunks.

She giggles again.

"What? What's so funny?"

"That one is for me."

"What?"

"The thing that made me laugh. It's only for me. I don't wanna tell it to anyone."

It Could Be
(Camroc Press Review, June 2012)

"What's this?" she said. But she knew.

"It's a dandelion."

"Yes. And what's this?" But she knew.

"It's another dandelion. Only with this one, you can blow off its little filaments. You know filaments?"

"Yes." But she didn't.

"It's called a dandelion clock. This one. The one you can blow off. They're like little parachutes."

"Yes. Little parachutes."

When she said "little" she pronounced the Ts slowly and carefully. I loved that.

"Do you know parachutes?"

"Yes." But she didn't. She handed me the small, yellow plant.

"This could be a little sunflower," she said.

"It could. It could be."

"Or…"

I let her think about it.

"…it could be just the Sun. The planet Sun."

"The *planet* Sun?"

"Yea."

"It could be."

"…smiling."

"Yes. Smiling at you."

"Or…"

I let her think.

"It could be the Moon."

"It could be."

She liked that. She liked the idea of it being the Moon.

"You can have this one. You can have the Moon."

I put the flower in my shirt pocket.

"I'll keep this until you come back to see me," I said.

"Yes. You can keep the Moon until I come back."

What she loved most was seeing the Moon in the daytime sky. She called it Luna. We had all kinds of good stories about Luna showing up in the daytime.

She would say: "...tell me about the story about how Luna follows us around with a slice of Swiss cheese."

And I'd pretend I didn't know that one, so she'd have to make it up, tripping over her words because her ideas were coming out too fast. Every time I prodded her, she'd make up a different story. And then I'd recount it back to her, only there was something fresh that she found in that, when I told it. Even though it was pretty much the same story, she loved hearing it from me.

Come on Livvy, let's go. Get strapped in. Your mum's here.

She climbed inside the back seat, still talking feverishly about something. She never stopped talking. I loved that. When the car pulled out, I could still see her mouth moving. I went inside and sat at the kitchen table. There was light coming in from behind me, shining on the French doors leading into the dining room. On the lower glass rectangles there were small prints, smudges really, of her tiny hands where she had pushed to open the doors. I took out the dandelion and set it on the counter, by the coffee machine. It had already wilted from the heat.

Some of Life
(The Bookends Review, August 2012)

There is nothing unusual about how we go at it. I'm up first. My morning cigarette. Up and turn the heater on. I hate the cold throughout the night. I hate sleeping in long sleeved shirts and trousers, but we cannot afford to run the machine for too long. I can stand winters here, though. They're short. Quite. Then I'm back in bed, body cold from the air outside on the balcony. We don't have an alarm. I just wake up. Sometimes she's up in the middle of the night. Sometimes I am. A few times. Neither one of us can sleep properly. She'll go read in the other room. I'll just lay there on my back running conversations with deceased friends or family. Talking in fragments. Writing in fragments.

Like:

"Joyce Carol Oates will give Balzac a run for his money."

"What?"

"She is the most prodigious writer out there."

"Prolific maybe."

Or looking for succubi sliding down the ceiling fan. And then I'll think: a grilled cheese sandwich. That'd be grand. A goddamned grilled cheese sandwich at three in the morning. With ketchup on the side. A huge dollop. I leave my watch on. When I sleep. Or even when I climb into the bath. She hates that. I hate it too but if I don't, I'll forget it. Everything is a routine. Even our drinking. Some mornings I sneak a mouthful of gin on my way out. When there is gin. I love leaving her in bed, knowing there is nothing she needs to do. But still. Neither of us sleeps. Nights come and they grind us down more than the days. And so there is nothing to ameliorate anything. Patches. Cheese. Rent. Wine. Melancholy.

"Leave the door open."

From the other room there is movement. Floor creaking. I'll sit and watch the sun come up. Most days. The light, more like. I never see the sun actually come up. We face north. And so it's like a dimmer being turned slowly. There is nothing unusual, really. There is the struggle. No answers. Rowing against the current.

Just people dying in an upper unit of a large, apartment complex. Not making any noise. Nullifying. No one will know we ever existed. And that's good.

"Wake me up at six."

"Why?"

"I want to talk with you."

The dimmer: on and off and on and off and on.

And off.

"Wake me up at six."

"Why?"

"I want to talk with you."

She shuffles her feet on the wood floor. It sounds like someone is sweeping. Away from me. She goes back to the room and pulls shut the drapes. I hear her settle in bed. She pushes her body into the soft mattress and changes sides until she falls asleep. I love that about her. She doesn't stop until she drifts.

My shift starts at seven and goes until five in the morning. Ten hours, four days a week. Only they're not consecutive. Monday night, Tuesday night, Wednesday off, Thursday night, Friday off, Saturday off, Sunday night. And it changes every week, the days I mean. I am never able to sleep properly. Neither is she.

We pass the days walking through fog and mist and the hot, July humid air, and we temper it with tequila and gin. It's how it goes. I love that. I love that we know exactly what is taking us down. There is no gallantry in that, just truth. I go to the kitchen and sit at the table with a little glass of clear Slivovitz. It's not the homemade stuff you get in the old country, but it does the job. It softens it all.

There are three books to get through and a stack of newspapers. Everything is still now. The five clocks ticking sound like someone is swinging slats of wood at the walls, in an urgent rage. I hear her shift in bed again. I hear her prop herself up on her elbow.

"Are you reading?"

"Yes."

"I'm sorry."

"It's all right. It's just the papers."

"I was thinking…let's go away."

"Go to sleep, you have a good hour."

"I can't. Let's just go away."

"Where?"

"Mexico. No. Cuba. Let's go to Cuba."

"Funny. I'm just reading that El Barbudo resigned."

"Who?"

"El Barbudo. The Bearded One."

"He did?"

"His brother took over. Nothing's really changed."

"Let's go anyway. Nothing's really changed in fifty years."

"We can't go from here. They won't let us."

"So we go from somewhere else."

"Go to sleep."

"We'll take a boat."

"Go already."

"I can't. I can't stop anything."

"Try."

"I can't."

"Just try."

It comes in from the sea, somehow. From the feet, and then slowly up the legs and the rest. We are both standing in the powdery sand with Rum and Chachaça cocktails and the music rushes up and envelops us.

"Ladies and gentlemen, Francesc d'Asís Xavier Cugat Mingall de Bru i Deulofeu!"

She takes a long hit and smiles.

"And singing with him, Miguelito Valdés!"

They go into a strange version of Perfidia. Ilsa and Rick are dancing to it in Paris. Then back to Cuba by way of Casablanca. Something lifts up from the hips and takes me back away from the waterfront. I watch the two of us still standing, listening to the musicians.

Then Cugat says:

I would rather play Chiquita Banana and have my swimming pool than play Bach and starve.

And we all applaud.

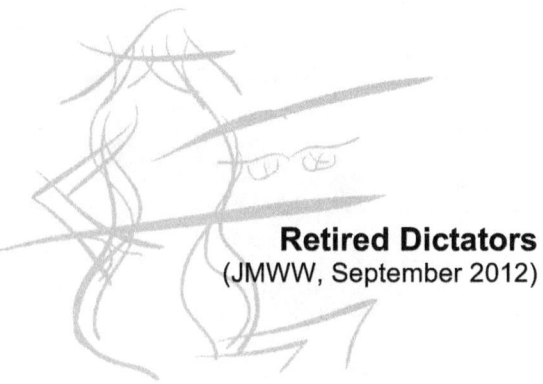

Retired Dictators
(JMWW, September 2012)

"I imagine this fate for them is worse than being in Hell," she said.

"Hell? What's that?"

She slapped me on the arm and called me Godless. I loved her, then. I loved her hair—half shaved off, the other, fiery red. I loved her leather jacket and black Doc Marten boots. I loved that she wore this getup no matter where she went, even at the beach. I loved her pasty white skin and the fact that whenever she walked, she literally jingled from the bracelets, the dog collars, and the chain she wore fastened to her wallet. But mostly I loved her because she did not love me back.

From within the garden we could see all the way out to The Charles Bridge and Slovansky Island. I felt the sophomoric urge just then to walk down to No. 22 Golden Lane and urinate on Kafka's house, to make some sort of primal, Alpha-Dog statement about mortality and worthiness. I was dumb.

"Well?"

"Well what?"

"Don't you think? Don't you think being trapped here like this is awful?"

"Seems like a good deal to me," I said. "It's green and peaceful and quiet; I'd take this over Hades."

She laughed and hit my arm again and said: "Hades! You don't believe in anything, do you?"

"I'm fond of Cerberus. Does that count?"

She did not answer. We walked solemnly around the giant, bronze beasts; they were all frozen in time by some ghastly Medusa who had tempted and dared, and then ensnared them all. Stalin's moustaches were soiled with bird shit, and someone had spray painted a penis on Lenin's crotch. The sculpted folds of his pants made the member look wavy and feeble and I supposed that was the intent. Tito and Ceausescu were there on their respective pedestals, looking regal and engaged in discourse, even though Ceausescu had been an illiterate cobbler with an awful speech impediment. I recognized Gottwald, Rákosi, and Gomułka…the lesser known monsters.

"It's quite sad, really," she said strolling around the gargantuan monuments like a bored ant. "They've all just been dumped here; just like that…like…abandoned cats."

"These men were horrible. You know that."

"I know…just…how it all ends up…it's sad. I mean, for all of us, really."

"In time, everything is forgotten. Nobody gives a shit. Everything fades and eventually is erased, just like Stalin used to order for those people purged from photographs. At least these animals get to live memorialized in a garden for a while."

"He did that?" She looked up at the thick, metal finger of Josef's right hand pointing across the grounds at the public toilets. "Stalin erased people from photographs?"

"The cover up was laughable," I said. "Anyone who was purged was literally rubbed out from the pictures in which they appeared. They did a terrible job, too. You could see the smudges and everything. Like a fucking four-year-old let loose with a gum eraser."

"That's awful."

"And laughable."

"Still…"

"We'll never have our own monuments; don't feel sorry for them. Look how satisfied they all are. It's a good life. Even suspended in the moment like this."

"They do look handsome…"

I loved her naïve empathy for these barbarians. I understood. I remember being sickened at the footage of Ceausescu's execution against the wall in that ordinary courtyard. He and his wife stood there looking like haggard feral animals waiting to be shot, and I felt badly for them, despite knowing the horrible methods of torture and death they had ordered for countless others. She kept calling the firing squad "my children" and implored them to reconsider. And when they went down, they both collapsed like deflated bags full of bones and bleeding organs.

"God, I have this weird desire to be kissed by the Brandenburg Gate."

I wanted to oblige her, but instead I just said: "You're in the wrong city."

"We should go. Thinking about all this is taking me low."

"I'm out of cigarettes; should we stop somewhere?"

"There's probably a tobacconist in Old Town Square, don't you think?"

"Probably."

"Tomorrow let's go to Prague Castle," she said. "I want to feel like a princess." She paused and thought for a moment; and then she redacted herself: "I want to know if I can feel like that."

In Our Time

"Hey, hey, no, no, no, no..." the one with the fancy moustaches barked and whistled through missing front teeth. He directed the operation in a type of controlled frenzy, arms flailing like an insane osprey, and somehow skillfully balancing the butt of a stale cigarette in the corner of his lips.

"Come, now come, come...come forward already!" he fired off directions to the others who were tugging on ropes and dripping from their foreheads into the dust, making small holes just next to their feet. "Bring, bring, bring...now ho' ho' ho'!" The crane inched forward, pulled laboriously by the men, all puffing on home rolled cigarettes. Everyone wore sandals. "Mind your toes, you donkeys!" Fancy Moustaches barked and laughed phlegmatically. His pertussis took hold just then, and he had to excuse himself during the cough attack.

"Look. Who is the true ass now," said one of the men, and the others smiled and slapped him on his back.

The crane was brought to the marked spot, secured, and balanced obtusely by the weight of six men acting as makeshift outriggers. They stood on floats—rectangular, wooden planks lined up to create a flat base for the human outriggers. "Bring forth the counterweights," Fancy Moustaches shot from in between his bouts of coughing. The others struggled with the irregular shapes of the rocks, but one by one they placed them on the back of the crane. The amount of counterweight needed for this particular lift was determined by Fancy Moustaches earlier. Inside a makeshift cafe, he calculated how many rocks it would take by resolving the weight of the load, the radius of the boom and the boom's angle during the operation.

The crowd swelled quickly. They were all men. They smoked and chatted and watched the workers prepare the crane for the lift. Some traded bags of fruit for other small objects and laughed. The boom of the crane began to telescope out, and upon seeing the hydraulics at work, the crowd burst into applause. Everyone was buzzing to see the operation. They formed a huge circle, several dozen men deep, around the area below the extended boom; cordoned off by Fancy Moustaches and his crew. The others, two men and a woman, were brought out by handlers. The woman was covered in a black burka. All three were hustled into the circular, improvised arena just underneath the boom.

"Hey...no, no, no, no, no," Fancy Moustaches spat out to one of his men like a Tommy Gun. "You must fit it backwards. Like so." He reached for the woman's shoulders and tugged, moving her close to his drenched face. He rearranged her until he was happy. "Like so...look, look, you donkey...watch me so you can learn." He grabbed hold of the noose and placed it backwards on the woman, so she would die slower. The other condemned souls, the men, would get nooses fitted the usual way, as a reward.

They strung up all three. The crowd suddenly became frenzied, shouting. The condemned men had their hands tied behind their backs. The woman's feet were shackled. The crowd erupted in a bizarre dissonance of anger, prayer, ridicule, and contemptuous screams. Some of the spectators looked possessed and shook their bodies as if spirits were revolting inside their breasts. The noose on the woman slipped out of position and a burly, bald man stepped out of the crowd and rearranged it. He smiled while he worked on her, and then spat on her, stepped back, and began to hop from one leg to the other.

Then they lifted them up by their necks and a roar went through the crowd. Some of them launched gobs of coagulated saliva at the condemned, as they were hoisted up like hunted animals. It was a ghastly way to die. They were being asphyxiated slowly. The men moved a little, soiled themselves, then they stopped. But the woman in the burka convulsed and struggled horribly. She kicked her legs repeatedly, violently, and contended like a fish out of water on a massive rod. After nearly five minutes, she stopped moving.

And then they all just dangled there, in the middle of the madness, while the crowd began to dance.

Love Removal Machine

The room in which the interview had been arranged to take place was an old fashioned antechamber—an empty vestibule with only two chairs facing one another across a wooden table with uneven legs. In a delicious coincidence, the small, brick building had been a church initially, then a funeral parlor for half a century, finally and unceremoniously auctioned to a mercurial arms dealer when the last of the mortuary family kin passed away childless. The weapons plutocrat subsequently opened a molecular gastronomy restaurant, which was used to funnel money to Gazneft TMK, the country's largest energy company, from petrol and natural gas derivatives sold with tremendous coercion to myriad gas franchises. After the businessman was found quartered and carefully packed into wooden crates bearing the logo of a major investment bank, the building was left abandoned, handed over to the erosion of city elements. It was here, in this ruinous venue that the Functionary agreed to speak with the Interviewer.

The two men sitting opposite one another looked like overgrown schoolboys bargaining for one another's lunchbox contents; each wearing a crisp, dark jacket with pressed white shirt, black tie, and handkerchief. The Interviewer scratched impatiently at an electronic tablet with an obtuse looking instrument that resembled an old fountain pen, but with short wires built into its bottom end. The screen of the tablet lit up, and cursive letters began to take shape beautifully as the man moved the implement across the glass screen.

"I am an obsessively precise fellow," the Functionary said. "Much like your calligraphy." His smile was not meant to excuse the idiosyncrasy but to reinforce it. "My kind of business cannot be run successfully in any other fashion. There are concrete rules by which we are governed. High rules."

The Interviewer paused, slid his bare finger across the screen, and highlighted a fragment of text he had just written.

"It's a kind of pun; a joke really," the Functionary said referring to the name of the service. "It has a...cult following, even." He paused for comedic effect, his thin lips forming a wry smile, but the Interviewer worked the pen furiously and missed the amusing reference.

"What we do is nothing different than running a retail business," the Functionary continued. "We work overnights, usually. Any day and every day; holidays and...rainy days and Mondays never get us down," he chuckled. The Interviewer either didn't seem to have any knowledge of the history of music, or he simply lacked a sense of humor.

"Although it's on weekends we see the most activity, as you may imagine. And Christmas and New Year's eves."

"Retail?"

"Well, yes. Or perhaps a utility might be a better analogy. We provide a necessary service. Like garbage removal or recycling pick up. The 'Machine' part refers to our ultra-efficient process. Rest assured, we are all...humans on staff."

The Interviewer shifted slightly, bumping into the foreshortened table, causing it to dislodge and rebalance itself on the three longer legs. The other man, visibly annoyed at the interruption, pressed on a corner and repositioned the table to its original spot. He kept pressure on the top to guard against repeating the wobbling motion that the Interviewer had inadvertently caused.

"What else would you like to know?" said the Functionary.

The question from the other man was delivered in a somewhat feeble and reluctant voice; that of an inquisitor with an initial upper hand (perhaps imagined), now quite shaken by a simple act of dominance and power established by his respondent in the previous moment. The Interviewer quickly realized the session now became a tricky game of power.

"We thrive on the misfortunes of the Roulette Player," the Functionary answered. "He is cursed with bad luck; even the one who lives long enough to attempt three bullets in the chamber. Oh yes, that happens quite frequently; all men are seduced by triumph over long odds and its payouts. If there is time, I will tell you about the unlucky one that survived the game playing with a fully loaded chamber. Indeed, survived.

"You see, these unfortunate men—and they are always men, trust me—divide themselves at the precise moment they raise the pistol to their temple. They measure the odds, one in six, two in six, sometimes three, and then divide themselves into their will and their chance. Their will to live—strong, resolute, at times misguided—seldom fails them, but their chance does not. Their chance runs faster and on sturdier legs. These men are not at all suicidal, like many assume. Their backbone and certitude are solid. They are positive. They want to conquer their fate. These men are deemed feckless, and so they are plucked from in between the layers of society, like harnessing roach eggs attached to glue on shelf liner. They are the downtrodden, the ones with angular faces, the sad donkeys. Most of them have no family, or if they do, it has excommunicated them to the life of the street or the underground sewage maze. Their worthlessness is exploited by Benefactors who, with a simple contract for a simple game of roulette, offer them the dream of inclusion into society again. They are told they could be respected citizens once more.

"Initial thoughts of merely owning practical items—a pair of shoes, trousers, a toothbrush—quickly mushroom into dreams of riches and comforts, power and, to most of these souls, retribution for their exile from humanity. You are surprised. It's true, the single, strongest motivator for this short-lived profession is Hate. Vendetta against the ones who castigated them...it is usually the catalyst for entering into such a contract with the Benefactors. You can see how a one in six chance of death, a chance that is much lower than the odds these men are facing in their lives on the street, stacked against an opportunity for revenge and a proper life again, a life full of possessions—albeit brief—can be so attractive to the Roulette Players. In fact, the six-to-one odds aren't that much higher than being crushed in an automobile accident."

"Really?"

The Interviewer quickly calculated his chances of returning to the office unharmed in the issued sedan. He skated over the glass surface of the tablet with his implement, furiously writing down notes. He took great care not to bump the table again; in fact, he took great care not to move at all.

"The end of the game is where we come in," the Functionary said. "The need for proper removal and disposal of losing players, as you may imagine, is vital. Discretion, efficiency, care, urgency, and respect are imperative. They are integral and inexorable to our business. But most of all, what we demand of our loyal staff is Love. They must fundamentally feel Love. Not necessarily for the details or mechanics of the job; please, forgive my cynicism...how often do we truly feel that? It is not a *job* if we love it, is it? And, given the nature of our business, the details of preparing and removing a body for disposal, not to mention the disposal itself, aren't the most attractive terms of the profession. Let's be frank.

"No, indeed one must love the losing players themselves. It is not required to dote on them in life—in fact we find it beneficial for our staff not to have had previous relations with these men, and if they do recognize a familiar face, we suggest they recuse themselves from that particular work order. Familiarity with our...clients breeds discrimination and preferential treatment, and we don't condone that. It is in our nature to treat those we've known with larger, softer kid gloves. And so we ask our staff to love these unknown men, these strangers, only in their death. In their death, they are beautiful and pure as infants. In their death they are born again...to *us*; they are new and fragile when they are delivered to us. We must cherish being entrusted with their quickly stiffening muscles.

"In all of our cases, we are the last to see the physical vessel; this elegant, intelligently designed, and often still bleeding organism now expeditiously decaying. As an aside, rigor mortis is extremely important in meat technology. The onset of rigor mortis and its resolution partially determines the tenderness of meat. If the post-slaughter meat is immediately chilled to 15°C, a phenomenon known as cold shortening occurs, where the muscle sarcomeres shrink to a third of their original length. But forgive me, I digress. Many blue moons ago I ran a butcher shop in what is now the city Armory."

"It seems like a logical segue into your profession," the Interviewer said.

"I'm happy you recognize that. The connection we have to flesh, whether living or dead, is inseparably attached to all of us, really. We indirectly create and quite bluntly destroy it. We worship it. Some societies even eat it. Ah, but I detect a twinge of disapproval. Not to worry my friend, I don't accede to cannibalism either. It goes against my moral disposition. I see your interest is now piqued. Your eyebrows give away your next question."

The Functionary chuckled. He kept pressure on the corner of the table. His eyes locked those of the Interviewer's only to have his connection broken.

"Please, don't be insulted," the Functionary said. "It is in the interest of our company's livelihood to anticipate and clarify questions on morality. Our political operatives often defend and explain our position to government representatives and ministers at the highest levels, opposed to the entire business of roulette. Yes, it is quite fierce in those hostile, private chambers of forged legislation; despite the tax revenues of the roulette. Lobbying for our political billet is part of our universe. It is nothing personal that I foresee your line of questioning. And I promise to deliver an unrehearsed answer. I am an honorable man; as honorable as I am precise."

The Functionary shifted his eyes to the Interviewer's handwriting on the tablet. It was, he thought, the perfect embodiment of a long lost classical art. The characters were historically disciplined yet fluid and spontaneous, at the moment of writing.

"The art of giving form to signs in an expressive, harmonious and skillful manner is truly formidable in our technological times," the Functionary said. "Quite impressive, really. And meritorious. I admire that in you."

The Interviewer stumbled into an awkward "Thank you."

"But you would like to know more about our moral position," the Functionary said, now sensing that the time was right to take full command of the session and advance his agenda.

"In particular, yours," the Interviewer said.

"Pardon?"

"I'd like to know about *your* moral principles."

Suddenly the Functionary felt struck with a jab from his blind side. His maneuvering for ground had been counterattacked. He felt backed into the corner, against the taut, nylon ropes burning channels across his bare shoulders. Disoriented, he absentmindedly let go of the table, which hung in balance briefly before tipping toward the other man.

"I am here as a representative of the firm," the Functionary said. "I assure you my personal beliefs are in line with those of all our operations and the high code of conduct by which we are governed." He stumbled through the response, his mind racing ahead, looking to anticipate his opponent's next few moves like he so thoroughly and accurately could in a game of chess. The balance of power had shifted.

"But only a few moments ago, while talking about cannibalism you mentioned how it goes against *your* moral disposition; that infers you are of different convictions from those of your firm's and its bylaws; I have it right here," the Interviewer scrolled up the screen of his electronic tablet. "I can show you..."

"No, it's all right. I'm quite aware of what I said. It was...an egregious syntaxical mistake to personalize moral values."

"Are you conflicted?"

There was a long pause. The Functionary's condition of Tinnitus, always present during stressful situations, interfered with his ability to respond quickly. He had slipped. He had made an error; he had left himself open to personal investigation.

"Would you like a break? I have a small bottle of water..." the Interviewer leaned down toward his field bag and began to unhook its top.

"Thank you, no. It's all right. Please, continue."

"We were about to explore your personal, moral position on what it is that you do for a living," said the Interviewer. The other man took a quick breath and began an attempt to rectify his mistake.

"Let me put this to you," the Functionary said. "When you think of the adjective *moral*, you find it synonymous with good or right, yes? Morality as you see it, is the *personal* differentiation of intentions and actions between those that are good, or right, and those that are bad, or wrong...such that immorality is the active opposition. Does that sound right?"

The Interviewer agreed.

"True," the Functionary said, "in its descriptive sense morality refers to personal or cultural values, codes of conduct, or social mores. It does not connote objective claims of right or wrong, but only refers to that which is *considered* right or wrong. However, in its normative sense morality refers to whatever, if anything, is actually right or wrong, which may be independent of the values held by any particular peoples or cultures."

"I am interested in the personal," the Interviewer said. "It's futile to examine morality in its normative sense, as you say; who can truly establish inflexible rules for morality to be followed in general and without deviation by others?"

"God can. And has."

The Interviewer stopped writing.

"God?"

The Functionary leaned back in his chair and said: "Indeed."

"Which God? Which version of God?"

"The only one. There is only one God," the Functionary said. "You are surprised."

"At your rigidity, yes. I find it hard to believe you fail to see the dozens of interpretations of God throughout religion."

"I don't fail to see them. I do refuse to recognize them. You cannot legitimize something that doesn't exist."

"Most people would turn that statement around to you."

"Most people are misguided."

"I didn't take you for a man of faith," the Interviewer said. He was intrigued and quite amused. "I imagined anyone involved in your line of work would be devoid of piety or the supernatural."

"Our business is governed by concrete rules; I've mentioned that," said the Functionary. "These rules apply as much to the theological details of our task, as to the technical. Sadly, what you are interested in, dear friend, is what's called tribal morality. Tribal morality is prescriptive, imposing the norms of the local collective on the individual. These norms are arbitrary, culturally dependent, and flexible. These norms are no more valuable than a list of home remedies for the common cold. They are wives tales. And they are extremely dangerous and exclusive. Distinct sets of moral rules apply to people depending on the membership of an in-group or an out-group. This is utter discrimination."

"It provides for group survival," the Interviewer said. "It's only logical. It's evolution."

"It's discriminatory, I must insist. Tribal morality breeds nationalism and patriotism. Both are forms of in-group/out-group boundaries. Both are concepts that have been failures to mankind."

"If you'll pardon me," the Interviewer said, "evolution *is* discriminatory. Quite. And with impunity."

"Evolution is sin," the Functionary cut in sharply. "Romans 1:25 clearly declares: 'They exchanged the truth of God for a lie, and worshipped and served created things rather than the Creator, who is forever praised. Amen.' My friend," the Functionary tried to control himself, "evolution is a faith-based system in regards to origins. We cannot go back to observe the origins of the universe or life in the universe. Evolution is an enabler for atheism. Evolution gives atheists a basis for explaining how life exists apart from a Creator God. Evolution denies the need for a God to be involved in the universe. Evolution is the 'creation theory' for the religion of atheism. According to the Bible, the choice is clear. We can believe the Word of our omnipotent and omniscient God, or we can believe the illogically biased, 'scientific' explanations of fools."

"But you must believe in science in some way," the Interviewer said. "Science has to be part of your process, your profession. Doesn't it?"

The Functionary chuckled.

"We are not embalmers. Our aim is not to preserve or forestall decomposition for later, public display. We are entrusted with the difficult task of acute, intelligent, and adept removal and disposal. We are really no more than a private service; a utility. But to answer your question, I acknowledge science...as a discipline of God's will."

"Do you administer last rites?"

"Sadly, the state in which we find our contracts makes it useless to give prayers and ministrations. These men are freshly departed. And no, I am not authorized to perform the sacred rituals. Nor is our firm authorized to employ any priests, were we to ever need them in the first place. As I've mentioned, we are governed by concrete rules. And the Ministry of Gaming, naturally."

The Functionary cleared his throat: "Allow me to tell you the story of the Roulette Player; a man so famous and revered for his bad fortune in the deadly game of roulette, that he survived playing for years, before he finally died from pistol, but not from bullet. I realize that sounds contradictory, but I will explain.

"Even then, at the height of his notoriety and misfortune, no one remembered his name. Of course he had one, but were you to inquire about him in the proper circles, no one would have been able to tell you what he was called. They all simply knew him as the Roulette Player. Before he took up the deadly but profitable game he was a gambler, and a degenerate at that. Horses, dogs, cockfighting, card games...anything that could be wagered upon, he tried and systematically failed miserably. Legends began to take shape about his life: he was a physicist, a banker, the winner of an incredible lottery pot, he was an executive with the country's largest energy company; anything that would explain his initial funds, which were squandered so beautifully and methodically. But that is just hearsay. People love to make up stories and build parables.

"Within months the Roulette Player became destitute and began to live underneath the city, in sewage tunnels. He subsisted on bits and scraps of vegetables, potato peels, eggshells, and other material pulverized by people's garbage disposals and plunged into the city's supply of wastewater, flowing in its bowels. From time to time he would surface; some claimed to have seen him in shady alleys looking for a pair of shoes or trousers, raiding waste containers, looking for discarded food...none of these appearances are verified, you understand. But what is certain is the reality of his misfortune.

"Like all the other parasitic supply of game product circulating within the intestines of a city, the Roulette Player was eventually chosen by a Benefactor to compete in a midnight game somewhere in the basement of a legitimate enterprise. Sensing this was his chance to engineer a macabre type of comeback, given his prior experience with luck, and looking at the six-to-one odds in his favor (the revolver used in these games is nearly always a six shooter), the Roulette Player took a one-night contract. His luck that first night earned him and his Benefactor an outrageous sum, for he was a cocky man and gambled in favor of his life six times during the gathering.

"From then, his career blossomed like a prokaryotic microorganism. With every game, his misfortune grew and solidified. I notice your confusion. Surely, you are thinking, I mean just the opposite. In the eyes of the Everyman, the Roulette Player was one of the luckiest men on earth. But you see, a man who continues to defy the odds time after time in the milieu of gambling is bad business for the House. The House cannot win all the time. And the Player...he couldn't lose. He was riddled with mischance. He would even play nine or ten games in one night, to the delight of his Benefactors and those who had placed wagers on his survival, naturally. In short time, he increased the frequency of his participation to a dozen, to a score, and then more, until he was playing in every scheduled bout, hours upon hours straight. Naturally, the Roulette Player became quite wealthy.

"But as the House cannot always win, he quickly turned into a liability to his Benefactors. Men stopped betting against him. Some even believed he was a type of deity; others called him a devil or demon. Soon, no one came. His Benefactors looked to other players—new blood from the sewers of the city. Something had to be done. And so it was he, the Roulette Player, who first suggested the idea of two bullets in the chamber.

"You see, he was a cocky man, and by that time he believed that fate was running so far behind him, it would never catch up. And so the crowds began to assemble again. Money flowed to his handlers. The stakes were high and seductive; two bullets in the chamber was a hit. But the Roulette Player's misfortunes continued. For he, again, beat the odds night after night. The familiar pattern of empty basements and warehouses resurfaced.

"And so again the stakes were raised: three bullets in the chamber. My friend, you are a highly intelligent man; you can guess where I am going with this. Four bullets. Five bullets. Until that spring night in March...when it was announced that the Roulette Player would use a fully loaded revolver; all six chambers housing the most deadly and beautiful lead alloy projectiles. This was the Roulette Player's masterpiece. It threw everyone into a frenzy. For there were many who thought the Player was of supernatural material, having survived the most narrow of odds time and time again, night after night. But there were just as many who refused to believe in mysticism. Imagine you, yourself, my friend. You are an intelligent man. You understand the absolute odds of such a peculiar situation. Surely you will wager at the very least a healthy sum of money on the overdue demise of the Roulette Player.

"There were men who came that night bearing the deeds to their houses, their cashed-in life insurance policies, inheritances, rights to various tracts of land, lifelong savings. You can imagine, my friend, what delicious temptation this must have been for a professional gambler. To a rational mind, there is no possibility of losing. For the first time in a gambler's life, the House held no odds in its favor.

"It was a glorious night. Men brought their wives. All were dressed to the nines. There was champagne and brandy served by waiters in crisp, white jackets. A string quartet played in the antechamber of the magnificent venue—a private mansion nestled among acres of oak trees. The stage itself was small; it only needed to accommodate one man. But what a man. What a horribly unlucky, beautiful man.

"At eleven o'clock the lights were dimmed in the soft, pulsating manner in which an opera hall might exercise, indicating the imminent start of the momentous event. The audience filed into the large manor hall quickly. There was a sinister air of anticipation; death, when expected or scheduled even, brings such an immense amount of anxiousness in its rucksack of potpourri and ball bearings, the chest of even an executioner begins to tighten exponentially with every minute closer to the deed. Imagine how the condemned man himself must feel. The crowd was high society people, champagne flutes held in delicate, fragile, soft hands, you understand. Many of them had never given the reality of the gruesome violence a game such as roulette carries a single thought. In fact, many of them were attending for the first time. They looked upon this night as a sporting event, a spectacle to which only fortunate ones were privy.

"The Roulette Player took his place unceremoniously; in fact, as he was dressed in a tuxedo himself, most audience members had no idea who he was. He came out into the chamber quickly from a side door; presumably the dressing room. It was only as he stepped up onto the small, rectangular podium that had been strategically placed in the middle of the hall that people realized who he was. Contrary to the stories you might hear, there wasn't much pomp and circumstance at all. There were no speeches made, nor any instructions or information given to those gathered. This was going to happen faster than a horse race. A small box holding the pistol was brought to the Player by a man resembling a waiter. The Player lifted the top, removed the weapon, slid open the empty chamber, and showed it to the room. He turned three hundred and sixty degrees to make sure everyone had a proper look. He then inserted all six bullets into their slots, presented the chamber to his audience once more like a careful magician, and slid it sideways, closed. Out of habit, or perhaps displaying a sense of humor on such a somber but exciting occasion, he gave the barrel a hefty spin, eliciting a few snickers from those experienced few in the crowd.

"No one moved or breathed, it seemed. The Roulette Player hesitated at what sounded like a deep moan coming from within the bowels of the edifice. But that only sidetracked his intentions momentarily. He raised the pistol to his temple. Another heavy moan was released, and this time everyone felt a strange vibration coming from below their feet. The Roulette Player was not to be distracted any longer. He pulled back the hammer.

"It was at this precise moment the Roulette Player, like all men taking part in this profitable game, divided himself into his will and his chance. Only, his will to live was no longer there. This Roulette Player had made up his mind long before this amazing event. His will fought against natural preservation. It fought against and transcended all instinct to live. And in the microsecond that was to decide his fate, chance intervened. His unfortunate luck caught him again. As the hammer came down, a gargantuan, guttural bellowing was heard, and the ground shook violently under everyone. The audience momentarily believed it heard the exaggerated echo of the gunshot. Men gasped. Some women screamed. The Player went down, as did most of those in attendance. The ground moaned and shook violently under everyone, bringing down everything that stood erect. It was the miracle of misfortune; the culmination of terrible luck. There had been an unprecedented, major earthquake.

"The bullet rushing out of the chamber merely grazed the Player's scalp on its way up toward the cracking, collapsing ceiling, as the angle of the barrel suddenly changed from the violent earth tremor, surging upwards instead of laterally into the fleshy temple. In an instant, after the shot, it was over. All things stopped shaking as if someone had ordered the chaos to cease. The earth became quiet and docile again, and an eerie silence fell on the ruined, dusty chamber. The crowd surged forward toward the awkward looking, shifted podium to find the Player slowly gathering and steadying himself up.

"A collective roar went up. It was a mixed, beastly cry of confusion, anger, and affirmation: from those in disbelief, from those furious at fate's intervention and the egregious sums of money it had cost them, and from those whose faith in an all-powerful God had just been reaffirmed. For there wasn't then, and certainly not since, any other explanation for this bizarre, seismic event, you understand. It came suddenly, at a precise moment in history, and disappeared in the same manner. Nothing like this had ever been recorded in this city. Nowhere in any sort of record kept is there a mention of ever having had an earthquake. This was God's will.

"The Roulette Player was never seen after that night. He may have very well gone back to the city underground sewage system where he rotted away among people's scraps of food. He had been killed by the pistol, you understand, but not by the bullet. From that moment on, no one ever wanted to have anything to do with him. He was poison to their vices—a demon, a fallen deity, a formidable enemy to gamblers. No one would dare bet against him ever again. His bad luck—being touched by the hand of God—engulfed him, smothered him. It saved him. It saved his soul.

"So you see, there is no other explanation," the Functionary said. "What happened that night can only be set in motion by a divine hand, don't you agree?"

The Interviewer raised his eyebrows in amusement and pushed out an incredulous smile as he wrote furiously on his tablet. The Functionary smiled as well. Inside, he felt a lightness of being that was immeasurable and indescribable. It was as if everything became illuminated, and a rush of adrenaline and endorphins flooded his blood vessels and invaded his head, briefly disorienting him and suddenly producing an euphoric state, which would remain within him for the duration of his life.

"So then," the Functionary regrouped. He gripped the foreshortened table and leaned hard on it, tipping it toward him, keeping pressure so it wouldn't rock back to its original position. "...you would like to know the technical details of our removal and disposal operations? I can give you those, if you wish; but off the record only. We are governed by strict laws, yes, but we are competitive. We wouldn't want to give away all our secrets to the competition."

"But that would be charity," the Interviewer said. "That's part of God's work, isn't it?"

One of the good legs of the foreshortened table gave a loud crack from the stress it was under, making the Functionary's face twitch slightly and quickly, just below the left eye.

ABOUT THE AUTHOR

Alex M. Pruteanu is the author of novella *Short Lean Cuts*.
Since emigrating to the United States from Romania in 1980,
he has worked as a journalist, television news director,
freelance writer, and editor. Alex lives with his family near
Raleigh, North Carolina.